"Do you like...children?" Lizzie shot at him, right out of the blue.

Already on red alert, Sebasten's defensive antennae lit up like the Greek sky at dawn. "Children are all right...at a distance," he pronounced, as cool as ice.

Lizzie lost every scrap of her natural color. "What sort of answer is that?"

"They can look quite charming in paintings," Sebasten conceded. "But they're noisy, demanding and an enormous responsibility. I'm much too selfish to want that kind of hassle in my life."

"I hope your future wife feels the same way" was all that Lizzie in her shattered state could think to mutter to cover herself in the hideous silence that stretched.

"I'm not planning to acquire one of those either," Sebasten confessed.

LYNNE GRAHAM

was born in Northern Ireland and has lived there all her life. She and her brother grew up in a seaside village. She now lives in a country house surrounded by a woodland garden, which is wonderfully private.

Lynne first met her husband when she was fourteen. They married after she completed her degree at Edinburgh University. Lynne wrote her first book at fifteen, and it was rejected everywhere. She started writing again when she was home with her first child. It took several attempts before she sold her first book and the delight of seeing that book for sale in the local store has never been forgotten.

Lynne always wanted a large family, and she has five children. Her eldest, and her only natural child, is in her twenties and is a university graduate. Her other children, who are every bit as dear to her heart, are adopted: two from Sri Lanka and two from Guatemala. In Lynne's home, there is a rich and diverse cultural mix, which adds a whole extra dimension of interest and discovery to family life.

The family has two pets: Thomas, a very large and affectionate black cat, and Daisy, an adorable but not very bright West Highland white terrier, who loves being chased by the cat. At night, dog and cat sleep together in front of the kitchen stove.

Lynne loves gardening, cooking, collecting everything from old toys to rock specimens and is crazy about every aspect of Christmas.

lynne graham

The Contaxis Baby

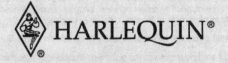

HARLEQUIN®

TORONTO • NEW YORK • LONDON
AMSTERDAM • PARIS • SYDNEY • HAMBURG
STOCKHOLM • ATHENS • TOKYO • MILAN • MADRID
PRAGUE • WARSAW • BUDAPEST • AUCKLAND

ISBN-13: 978-0-373-19881-8
ISBN-10: 0-373-19881-7

THE CONTAXIS BABY

This edition published by arrangement with Harlequin Books S.A.

® and TM are trademarks of the publisher. Trademarks indicated with ® are registered in the United States Patent and Trademark Office, the Canadian Trade Marks Office and in other countries.

www.eHarlequin.com

Printed in U.S.A.

CHAPTER ONE

WHEN Sebasten Contaxis strode to Ingrid Morgan's side to offer his condolences on the death of her only son, she fell on his chest and just sobbed as though her heart had broken right through.

A ripple of curiosity ran through the remaining guests in the drawing room of the Brighton town house. The tall, powerfully built male, every angle of his bronzed features stamped with strength and authority, looked remarkably like...but surely not? After all, what could be the connection? Why would the Greek electronics tycoon come to pay his respects *after* Connor's funeral? But keen eyes picked out the long, opulent limousine double-parked across the street and then judged the two large men waiting on the pavement as the bodyguards that they were. Heads turned, moved closer together and the whispers started.

Stunning dark eyes veiled, Sebasten waited until Ingrid had got a grip on that first outburst of grief before murmuring, 'Is there anywhere that we can talk?'

'Still looking after my good name?' Ingrid lifted her blonde head and he tensed at the sight of the raw suffering etched in her once beautiful features. Then he knew that even her love for his late father had in the end been surpassed by her devotion to her son. 'It doesn't really matter now, does it? Connor's gone where he can never be embarrassed by my past...'

She took him into an elegant little study and poured drinks for them both. Always slim, right now she looked emaciated and every day of her fifty-odd years. She had been his father's mistress for a long time and some of the few happy childhood memories Sebasten had related to her and Connor, who had been five years his junior. For all too short a spell, Connor had been the kid brother he had never had, tagging after Sebasten on the beach, a little blond boy, cheerfully and totally fearless. As an adult, he had become a brilliant polo player, adored by women, in fact very popular with both sexes. Not the brightest spark on the block but a very likeable guy. Yet it had been well over a year since Sebasten had last seen the younger man.

'It was murder, you know…' Ingrid condemned half under her breath.

Sebasten's winged dark brows drew together but he remained silent, for he had heard the rumour that Connor's car crash had been no accident, indeed, a deliberate act of self-destruction, and he knew that there was no more painful way to lose a loved one. She needed to talk and he knew that listening was the kindest thing he could do for her.

'I liked Lisa Denton…when I met that evil little shrew, I actually *liked* her!' Ingrid proclaimed with bone-deep bitterness.

The silence lay before Ingrid continued in a tremulous tone. 'I knew Connor was in love when he stopped confiding in me. That hurt but he was twenty-four…that's why I didn't pry.'

'Lisa Denton?' Sebasten was keen to deflect her from that unfortunate angle.

Her stricken blue eyes hardened. 'A spoilt little rich brat. Gets her kicks out of encouraging men to make an ass of themselves over her! It's only three months since Connor met her but I could tell he'd fallen like a ton of bricks.' The older woman swallowed with visible difficulty. 'Then without any warning, *she* got bored. She cut him dead at a party two weeks ago…made an exhibition of herself with another man, laughed in his face…his friends told me *everything*!'

Sebasten waited while Ingrid gathered her shredded composure back together again.

'He begged but she wouldn't even take a phone call from him. He'd done nothing. He couldn't handle it,' Ingrid sobbed brokenly. 'He wasn't sleeping, so he went for a drive in his car in the middle of the night and drove it into a wall!'

Sebasten curved an arm round her in a consoling embrace and seethed with angry distaste at the ugly picture she had drawn up. Connor would have been soft as butter in the hands of a manipulative little bitch like that.

'You're going to hate me for what I t-tell you now...' Ingrid whispered shakily.

'Nonsense,' Sebasten soothed.

'Connor was your half-brother...'

Sebasten released his breath in a sudden startled hiss and collided with Ingrid's both defiant and guilty gaze.

'No...that's not possible,' he breathed in total shock, not wanting it to be true when it was too late for him to do anything about it.

Ingrid sank down in a distraught heap and sobbed out a storm of self-justification while Sebasten stared at her as though he had never seen her before. She had never told his father, Andros, because she had known how ruthless Andros would be at protecting the good name of the Contaxis family from scandal.

'If Andros had known, he would've bullied me into having a termination. So I left him, came back eighteen months later, confessed to a rebound relationship, *grovelled*...eventually he took me back!' For a frozen instant in time, Ingrid's face shone with the remembered triumph of having fooled her powerful lover and then her eyes, fell, the flash of energy draining away again.

'How could you not tell me before this?' Sebasten bit out in an electrifying undertone, lean, strong face rigid with the force of his appalled incredulity. In the space of seconds, Connor's death had gone from a matter of sincere and sad regret to a tragedy which gutted Sebasten. But he knew why, knew all too well why she had kept quiet. Fear of the consequences would have kept her quiet throughout all the years she had loved his father without adequate return.

'I'm only telling you now because I want you to make Lisa Denton sorry she was ever born...' Ingrid confided with harsh clarity as his brilliant gaze locked to her set features and the hatred she could not hide. 'You're one of the richest men on this planet and I don't care how you do it. There have got to be strings you could pull, pressure you could put on somewhere with someone to *punish* her for what she did to Connor...'

'No,' Sebasten murmured without inflection, a big, dark, powerful Greek male, over six feet four in height and with shimmering dark golden eyes as steady as rock. 'I am a Contaxis and I have honour.'

Minutes later, Sebasten swept out of Ingrid's home, impervious to the lingering mourners keen to get a second look at him. In the privacy of his limo, he sank a double whiskey. His lean, dark, handsome face was hard and taut and ashen pale. He had no doubt that Ingrid had told him the truth. Connor...the little brother he had only run into twice at polo matches in recent years. He might have protected him from his own weakness but he hadn't been given the chance. Certainly, he could have taught him how to handle *that* kind of woman. Had Lisa Denton found out that, in spite of his popularity and his wealthy friends, Connor was essentially penniless but for his winnings on the polo field? Or had Connor's puppy-dog adoration simply turned her off big time? His wide, sensual mouth curled. Was she a drop-dead babe who treated men like trophies?

He pitied Ingrid for the bitterness that consumed her. Yet even after all those years in Greece, she *still* hadn't learned that one essential truth: a man never discussed family honour with a woman or involved her in certain personal matters...

*   *   *

Maurice Denton stared out of his library window and then turned round to face his daughter, his thin, handsome face set with rigid disapproval.

'I can't excuse *anything* you've done,' he asserted.

Lizzie was so white that her reddish-blonde hair seemed to burn like a brand above her forehead. 'I didn't ask you to,' she murmured unevenly. 'I just said…we all make mistakes…and dating Connor was mine.'

'There are standards of decent behaviour and you've broken them,' the older man delivered as harshly as if she hadn't spoken. 'I'm ashamed of you.'

'I'm sorry.' Her voice wobbled in spite of all her efforts to control it but that last assurance had burned deep. 'I'm really…*sorry*.'

'It's too late, isn't it? What I can't forgive is the public embarrassment and distress that you've caused your stepmother. Last night, Felicity and I should have been dining with the Jurgens but it was cancelled with a flimsy excuse. As word gets around that your cruelty literally *drove* the Morgan boy to his death, we're becoming as socially unacceptable as you have made yourself—'

'Dad—'

'Hannah Jurgen was very fond of Connor. A lot of people were. Felicity was extremely upset by that cancellation. Indeed, from the minute the details of this hideous business began leaking into the tabloids Felicity has scarcely slept a night through!' Maurice condemned fiercely.

Pale as milk, Lizzie turned her head away, her throat tight and aching. She might have told him that his young and beautiful wife, the woman who was the very centre of his universe, couldn't sleep for fear of exposure. But what right did she have to play God with his marriage? She asked herself painfully. What right did she have to speak and destroy that marriage when the future security of her own little unborn brother or sister was also involved in the equation?

'Do you think it's healthy for a pregnant woman to live

in this atmosphere and tolerate being cold-shouldered by
those she counted as friends just because you've made
yourself a pariah?' her father demanded in driven contin-
uance.

'I broke off my relationship with Connor. I didn't do
anything else.' Even as Lizzie struggled to maintain her
brittle composure she was trembling,.for she was not accustomed to hearing that cold, accusing tone from her father, and in her hurt and bewilderment she could not find
the right words to try and defend her own actions. 'I'm
not to blame for his death,' she swore in a feverish protest.
'He had problems that had nothing to.do with me!'

'This morning, Felicity went down to the cottage to
rest,' the older man revealed with speaking condemnation.
'I want my wife home by my side where she ought to be.
Right now, she needs looking after and my first loyalty
lies with her and our unborn child. For that reason, I've
reached a decision, one I probably should have made a
long time ago. I'm cutting off your allowance and I want
you to move out.'

Shock shrilled through Lizzie, rocking what remained
of her once protected world on its axis: she was to be
thrown to the wolves for her stepmother's benefit. She
stared in sick disbelief at the father whom she had adored
from childhood, the father whom she had fought to protect
from pain and humiliation even while her own life disin-
tegrated around her.

Maurice had always been a loving parent. But then the
death of Lizzie's mother when she was five and the fifteen
years that had passed before the older man remarried had
ensured that father and daughter had a specially close
bond. But from the day he had met Felicity, brick by brick
that loving closeness had been disassembled. Felicity had
ensured that she received top billing in every corner of her
husband's life and his home.

'Believe me, I don't mean this as a punishment. I hope
I'm not that foolish,' the older man framed heavily. 'But

it's obvious that I've indulged and spoilt you to a degree where you care nothing for the feelings of other people—'

'That's not true...' Lizzie was devastated by that tough assessment.

'I'm afraid it is. Making you go out into the world and stand on your own feet may well be the kindest thing I can do for you. There'll be no more swanning about at charity functions in the latest fashions, kidding yourself on that that's real work—'

'But I—'

'—and after the manner of Connor's death, who is likely to invite you to talk about generosity towards those less fortunate?' Maurice enquired with withering bite. 'Your very presence at a charity event would make most right-thinking people feel nauseous!'

As the phone on the desk rang, Lizzie flinched. Her father reached for it and gave her a brusque nod of finality, spelling out the message that their meeting was at an end. The distaste he could barely hide from her, the angry shame in his gaze cut her to the bone. She stumbled out into the hall and made her way back to the sanctuary of her apartment, which lay behind the main house in what had once been the stable block.

For a while, Lizzie was just numb with shock. Over the past ten days, shock had piled on shock until it almost sent her screaming mad. Yet only a fortnight ago, she had been about to break the news of the fabulous surprise holiday in Bali she had booked for Connor's birthday. She had not even managed to cancel that booking, she acknowledged dimly, must have lost every penny of its considerable cost. But then when had she ever had to worry about money? Or running up bills on her credit card because she had overrun her monthly allowance? Now, all those bills would have to be paid...

But what did that matter when she had lost the man she had loved to her own stepmother? Sweet, gushy little Felicity, who was so wet she made a pond look dry. Yet

Felicity, it seemed, had also been the love of Connor's life and, finally rejected by her, he had gone off the rails.

'I didn't mean it to happen…I couldn't help myself!' Connor had proclaimed, seemingly impervious to the consequences of the appalling betrayal he had inflicted on Lizzie. The guy she had believed was her best friend ever, maybe even her future husband, and all the time he'd just been using her as a convenient cover for his rampant affair with her stepmother—the whiny, weepy Felicity! A great, gulping sob racked Lizzie's tall, slender frame and she clamped a hand to her wobbling mouth. She caught an unwelcome glimpse of herself in the mirror and her bright green eyes widened as she scanned her own physical flaws. Too tall, too thin with not a shadow of Felicity's feminine, sexy curves. No wonder Connor had not once been tempted all those weeks…

And Connor? Her tummy twisted in sick response. What a ghastly price he had paid for his affair with a married woman! Connor…dead? How could she truly hate him when he was gone? And how could she still be so petty that she was feeling grateful that she had never got as far as offering her skinny body to Connor in some ludicrous romantic setting in Bali? He would have run a mile!

Mrs Baines, the housekeeper, appeared in the doorway looking the very picture of discomfiture. 'I'm afraid that your father has asked me to pack for you.'

'Oh…' In the unkind mirror, Lizzie watched all her freckles stand out in stark contrast to her pallor before striving to pin an unconcerned expression to her face to lessen the older woman's unease. 'Don't worry about it. I'm all grown now and I'll survive.'

'But putting you out of your home is *wrong*,' Mrs Baines stated with a sharp conviction that startled Lizzie, for, although the housekeeper had worked for the Dentons for years, she rarely engaged in conversation that did not relate to her work and had certainly never before criticised her employer.

'This is just a family squabble.' Lizzie gave an awkward shrug, touched to be in receipt of such unexpected support but embarrassed by it as well. 'I…I'm going for a shower.'

Closeted in the bathroom, she frowned momentarily at the thought of that surprising exchange with Mrs Baines before she stabbed buttons on her mobile and called Jen, her closest remaining female friend. 'Jen?' she asked with forced brightness when the vivacious blonde answered. 'Could you stand a lodger for a couple of days? Dad's throwing me out!'

'Are you jossing me?'

'No, talking straight. Right at this very moment, our housekeeper is packing for me—'

'With your wardrobe…I mean, you *are* the original shop-till-you-drop girl; she'll still be packing at dawn!' Jen giggled. 'Come on over. We can go out and drown your sorrows together tonight.'

At that suggestion, Lizzie grimaced. 'I'm not in a party mood—'

'Take it from me, you *need* to party. Stick your nose in the air and face down the cameras and the pious types. There, but for the grace of God, go I!' Jen exclaimed with warming heat only to spoil it by continuing with graphic tactlessness, 'You ditched the guy…you were only with him a few months, like how does that make *you* responsible for him getting drunk and smashing himself up in his car?'

Lizzie flinched and reflected that Jen's easy hospitality would come with a price tag attached. But then, where else could she go in the short term? People had stopped calling her once the supposed truth of Connor's 'accident' had been leaked by his friends. She just needed a little space to sort out her life and, with the current state of her finances, checking into a hotel would not be a good idea. Maybe Jen, whose shallowness was legendary, would cheer her up. Maybe a night out on the town would lift her out of her growing sense of shellshocked despair.

* * *

'Work?' Jen said it as if it was a dirty word and surveyed Lizzie with rounded eyes of disbelief as she led the way into a bedroom mercifully large enough to hold seven suit-cases and still leave space to walk around the bed. '*You…work?* What at? Stay with me until your father calms down. Just like me, you were raised to be useless and decorative and eventually become a wife, so let's face it, it's hardly your fault.'

'I'm going to stand on my own feet…just as Dad said,' Lizzie pronounced with a stubborn lift of her chin. 'I want to prove that I'm not spoilt and indulged—'

'But you *are*. You've never done a proper day's work in your life!' A small, voluptuous blonde, Jen was never seen with less than four layers of mascara enhancing her sherry-brown eyes. 'If you take a job, when would you find the time to have your hair and nails done? Or meet up with your friends for three-hour lunches or even take off at a moment's notice for a week on a tropical beach? I mean, it would be *gruesome* for you.'

Faced with those realities, it truly did sound a gruesome prospect to Lizzie too, although she was somewhat re-sentful of her companion's assertion that she had *never* worked. She had done a lot of unpaid PR work for charities and had proved brilliant at parting the seriously wealthy from their bundles of cash with stories of suffering that touched the hardest hearts. She had sat on several com-mittees to organise events and, well, *sat* there, the ultimate authority on how to make a campaign look cool for the benefit of those to whom such matters loomed large. But nine-to-five work hours, following orders given by other people for some pocket-change wage, no, she hadn't ever done that. However, that didn't mean that she *couldn't*…

Four hours later, Lizzie was no longer feeling quite so feisty. Whisked off to the latest 'in' club, Lizzie found herself seated only two tables from a large party of former friends set on shooting her filthy looks. She was wearing an outfit that had been an impulse buy and a mistake and, in addition, Jen had been quite short with her when she had had only two alcoholic drinks before trying to order her usual orange juice. Reluctant to offend the blonde, who felt just then like her only friend in the world, Lizzie was now drinking more vodka.

'When my girlfriends won't drink with me, I feel like they're acting superior,' Jen confessed with a forgiving grin and then threw back a Tequila Sunrise much faster than it could have been poured.

When Jen went off to speak to someone, Lizzie went to the cloakroom. Standing at the mirrors, she regretted having allowed Jen to persuade her to wear the white halter top and short skirt. She felt too exposed yet she often bought daring outfits even though she never actually wore them. While she was wondering why that was so, she overheard the chatter of familiar female voices.

'I just can't *believe* Lizzie had the nerve to show herself here tonight!'

'But it does prove what a heartless, self-centred little—'

'Tom's warning Jen that if she stays friendly with Lizzie, she's likely to find herself out on her own with *only* Lizzie!'

'How could she have treated Connor that way? He was so much fun, so kind…'

Lizzie fled with hot, prickling tears standing out in her shaken eyes. Returning to her table, she drained her glass without even tasting the contents. Those female voices had belonged to her friends. One of them had even gone to school with her. *Ex-friends.* All of a sudden everybody hated her, yet only weeks ago she had had so many invitations out she would have needed a clone of herself to attend every event. Now she wanted to bolt for the exit and go home. But she wasn't welcome at home any more and Jen would be furious if she tried to end the evening early.

Yes, Connor had seemed kind. At least, she had thought

so too until she went down to the Denton country cottage and found Connor in bed with Felicity. Her skin turned cold and clammy at that tormenting memory.

She had been thinking about inviting a bunch of friends to the cottage for the weekend. Believing that the property had been little used in recent times, she had decided to check out that there would be sufficient bedding. Connor must have come down from London in her stepmother's car and it had been parked out of sight behind the garage, so Lizzie had had no warning that the cottage was occupied. She had been in a lovely, bubbly mood, picturing how amazed Connor would be when she told him that he would be spending his twenty-fifth birthday in Bali.

Lizzie had been on the stairs when she heard the funny noises: a sort of rustling and moaning that had sent a momentary chill down her spine. But even at that stage she had not, in her ignorance, suspected that what she was hearing was a man and a woman making love. Blithely assuming that it was only the wind getting in through a window that had been left open, she had gone right on up. From the landing, she had got a full Technicolor view of her boyfriend and her stepmother rolling about the pine four-poster bed in the main bedroom.

Felicity had been in the throes of what had looked more like agony than ecstasy. Connor had been gasping for breath in between telling Felicity how much he loved her and how he couldn't bear to think that it would be another week before he could see her again. Throughout that exchange, Lizzie had been frozen to the spot like a paralysed peeping Tom. When Felicity had seen her, her aghast baby-blue eyes had flooded with tears, making her look more than ever like a victim in the guise of a fairytale princess.

But then crying was an art form and a way of life for her stepmother, Lizzie reflected, striving valiantly to suppress the wounding images she had allowed to surge up from her subconscious. Felicity wept if dinner was less than perfect… 'It's my fault…it's my fault,' she would fuss until Maurice Denton was on his knees and promising her a week in Paris to recover from the trauma of it. In much the same way and with just as much sincere feeling she had wept when Lizzie found her in bed with Connor Morgan. Tears had dripped from her like rain but her nose hadn't turned red and her eyes hadn't swelled up pink.

When Lizzie cried, it was noisy and messy and her skin turned blotchy. That afternoon, Connor and Felicity had enjoyed a full performance to that effect, before Lizzie's pride came to the rescue and she told them to get out of the cottage. After they had departed, she had made a bonfire of their bedding in the back garden. Recalling that rather pointless exercise, she forced herself upright with an equally forced smile when Jen urged her up to dance.

Up on the overhanging wrought-iron gallery above, Sebasten was scanning the crowds below while the club manager gushed by his side, 'I recognised the Denton girl when she arrived. She looks a right little goer…'

Derisive distaste lit Sebasten's brooding gaze. The very fact that Lisa Denton was out clubbing only forty-eight hours after the funeral told him *all* he needed to know about the woman who had trashed Connor's life.

'Although *little* wouldn't be the operative word,' the older man chuckled. 'She's a big girl…not even that pretty; wouldn't be my style anyway.'

His companion's inappropriate tone of prurience gritted Sebasten's even white teeth. Beyond the fact that he had a very definite need to put a face to the name, he had no other immediate motive for seeking out Lisa Denton. She would pay for what she had done to Connor but Sebasten never acted in reckless haste and invariably employed the most subtle means of retribution against those who injured him.

At that point, his attention was ensnared by the slender woman spinning below the lights on the dance floor below, long hair the colour of marmalade splaying in a sea of amber luxuriance around her bare shoulders. She flung her head back with the kind of suggestive abandonment that fired a leap of pure adrenalin in Sebasten. Every muscle in his big, powerful length snapped taut when he saw her face: the exotic slant of her cheekbones below big, faraway eyes and a lush, full-lipped pink mouth. Her beauty was distinctive, unusual. Her white halter-neck top glittered above a sleek, smooth midriff and she sported a skirt the tantalising width of a belt above lithe, shapely legs that were at least three feet long. Bloody gorgeous, Sebasten decided, sticking out an expectant hand for the drink he had ordered and receiving it while contemplating that face and those legs and every visible inch that lay between with unashamed lust and wholly dishonourable intentions. Tonight, he would *not* be sleeping alone…

'That's *her*…the blonde…'

Recalled to the thorny question of Lisa Denton by his companion's pointing hand, Sebasten looked to one side of *his* racy lady with the marmalade hair and, seeing a small blonde with the apparent cleavage of the Grand Canyon, understood why the manager had referred to his quarry as a big girl. So *that* was the nasty little piece of work whom Connor had lost his head over. Sebasten was not impressed but then he hadn't wanted or expected to be.

On the dance floor below, Jen touched Lizzie's shoulder to attract her attention. Only then did Sebasten appreciate that the two women knew each other and he frowned, for such a close connection could prove to be a complication. It was predictable that within the space of ten seconds Sebasten had worked out how that acquaintance might even benefit his purpose.

Jen reached the table she had been seated at with Lizzie first and then turned with compressed lips. 'I've been thinking that…well, perhaps it's not such a good idea for you to stay with me…'

Remembering the dialogue that she had overheard in the

cloakroom, Lizzie felt her heart sink. 'Has someone been getting at you?'

'Let's be cool about this,' Jen urged with a brittle smile. 'I have every sympathy for the situation you're in right now but I have to think of myself too and I don't want to—'

'Get the same treatment?' Lizzie slotted in.

Jen nodded, grateful that Lizzie had grasped the point so fast. 'You should just go to a hotel and keep your head down for a while. You can pick up your things tomorrow. By this time next week, everybody will have found something other than Connor to get wound up about.'

And with that unlikely forecast, Jen walked without hesitation into the enemy camp two tables away and sat down with the crowd, who had been ignoring Lizzie all evening. For an awful instant, Lizzie was terrified that she was going to break down and sob like a little baby in front of them all. Whirling round, she pushed her way back onto the crowded dance floor, where at least she was out of view.

It was an effort to think straight and then she stopped trying, just sank into the music and gave herself up to the pounding beat. Her troubled, tearful gaze strayed to the male poised on the wrought-iron stairs that led down from the upper gallery and for no reason that she could fathom she fell still again. He was tall, black-haired and possessed of so striking a degree of sleek, dark good looks that the unattached women near by were focusing their every provocative move on him and even the attached ones were stealing cunning glances past their partners and weighing their chances.

He looked like a child in a toy shop: spoilt for choice while he accepted all those admiring female stares as his due. He was also the kind of guy who never looked twice at Lizzie except to lech over her legs and then wince at her flat chest and her freckles when he finally dragged his Neanderthal, over-sexed gaze up that high. Story of my life, Lizzie conceded. An over-emotional sob tugged at her throat as self-pity demolished a momentarily entrancing fantasy of said guy making a beeline for her and thoroughly sickening Jen and her cohort of non-wellwishers.

Ashamed of her own emotional weakness, Lizzie headed for the bar, for want of anything better to do.

A hand suddenly closed over hers, startling her. 'Let me…' a dark, deep, sinfully rich drawl murmured in her ear.

Let him…*what*? Flipping round, Lizzie had the rare experience of having to tilt her head back to look up at a man. She encountered stunning dark golden eyes and stopped breathing, frozen in her tracks by shock. It was the guy from the stairs and close to he was even more spectacular than he had looked at a distance, not to mention being very much taller than she had imagined. Male too, very, *very* male, was the only other description she could come up with as she simply stared up at him.

Beneath her astonished scrutiny, he snapped long brown fingers, tilted his arrogant dark head back to address someone out of view and then began to walk her away from the crush at the bar again.

'I've got freckles…' Lizzie mumbled in case he hadn't noticed.

'I shall look forward to counting them.' He flashed her the kind of smile that carried a thousand megawatts of sheer masculine charisma and her heart, her *dead* and battered heart, leapt in her chest as though she had been kicked by an electrical charge.

'You *like* freckles?'

'Ask me tomorrow,' Sebasten purred with husky amusement.

CHAPTER TWO

As Sebasten approached the table where Lizzie had been seated, his bodyguards, who Lizzie assumed were bouncers, shifted the people about to take it over with scant ceremony. Two waiters then appeared at speed to clear the empty glasses.

Watching that ruthless little display of power being played out before her, Lizzie blinked in surprise. Was he the manager or the owner of the club? Who else could he be? The bar was heaving with a crush of bodies but the bouncer types only had to signal to receive a tray of drinks while others less influential fumed.

Looking across the table as her companion folded down with athletic grace into a seat, Lizzie still found herself staring: he was just *so* breathtaking. His lean, bronzed features were framed with high cheekbones, a narrow-bridged classic nose and a stubborn jawline. He had the kind of striking bone structure that would impress even when he was old. Luxuriant black hair curled back from his forehead above strong, well-marked brows, his brilliant, deepset dark eyes framed by thick black lashes. Her heart hammered when he smiled at her again but she could not shake the lowering sensation that his choice of her with her less obvious attractions was a startling and inexplicable event.

'I'm Sebasten,' Sebasten drawled, cool as glass. 'Sebasten Contaxis.'

His name meant nothing to Lizzie but, as what she had already seen suggested that she *ought* to recognise the name, she nodded as if she had already recognised him and, having finally picked up on the sexy, rasping timbre

21

of his accent, said, 'I'm Lizzie…you're not from London—er—originally, are you?'

Taking that as a case of stating the obvious with irony, Sebasten laughed. 'Hardly, but I'm very fond of this city, Lizzie? Short for? The obvious?'

'Yes, after my mother…it's what my family and closest friends call me.' As Lizzie met the concentrated effect of those spectacular dark golden eyes, a *frisson* of feverish tension not unlaced with alarm seized her: he was not the sort of straightforward, safe male she was usually drawn to. There was danger in the aura of arrogant expectation he emanated, in the tough strength of purpose etched in that lean, dark, handsome face. But perhaps the greatest threat of all lay in the undeniable sizzle of the sexual signals in that smouldering gaze of his.

'I take it that you saw at one glance that we were likely to be close,' he said in a teasing undertone that sent a potent little shiver down her taut spine.

Her breath snarled up in her throat. Caution urged her to slap him down but she didn't want him to walk away, could not, at that instant, think of clever enough words with which to gracefully spell out the reality that she was not into casual intimacy on short acquaintance. But for the first time in her life, Lizzie realised that she was seriously *tempted* and that shook her.

In surprise, Sebasten watched the hot colour climb in her cheeks so that the freckles all merged, the sudden downward dip of her eyes as she tilted her head to one side in an evasive move that was more awkward than elegant. For a moment, in spite of her sophisticated, provocative appearance, she looked young, *very* young and vulnerable.

'Smile…' he commanded, suddenly wondering what age she was.

And her generous mouth curved up as if she couldn't help herself in an entirely natural but rather embarrassed grin that had so much genuine appeal that Sebasten was entrapped by the surprise of it. 'I'm not the best company tonight,' she told him in a tone of earnest apology.

Sebasten rose in one fluid movement to his full height and extended a hand. 'Let's dance...'

As Lizzie got up she caught a glimpse of the staring faces at that table of ex-friends that she had been avoiding all evening and she threw her head back, squaring her taut bare shoulders. It felt good to be seen with a presentable male, rather than being alone and an object of scornful pity.

Just as it had once felt good to be with Connor? Lizzie snatched in a sharp gasp of air, painfully aware that Connor had smashed her confidence to pieces. She had thought that he was as straight and honest as she was herself. When he had made no attempt to go beyond the occasional kiss, she had believed his plea that he *respected* her and wanted to get to know her better. In retrospect that made her feel such an utter and naïve fool, for his restraint had encouraged her to make all sorts of foolish assumptions, not least the belief that he was really serious about her. When she was forced to face the awful truth that Connor had instead been sleeping with her much more beautiful stepmother, she had been devastated by her own trusting stupidity.

A strong arm curved round Lizzie and tugged her close in a smooth move that brought her into glancing collision with Sebasten's lean, muscular length. A shockwave of heated response slivered through her quivering body.

'What age are you?' Sebasten demanded, an aggressive edge to his deep, dark drawl, for he had seen the distant look in her eyes and he was unaccustomed to a woman focusing on anything other than him.

Putting that tone down to the challenge of competing against the backdrop of the pounding music, Lizzie told him, 'Twenty-two...'

'Taken?' Sebasten prompted, a primal possessiveness scything up through him at the sudden thought that she might well be involved with some other man and that that was the most likely explanation for her total lack of flirtatiousness.

He was holding her close on a floor packed with people all dancing apart but as Lizzie looked up into his burnished lion-gold eyes she was only aware of the mad racing of her own heartbeat and the quite unfamiliar curl of heat surging up inside her.

'Taken?' she queried, forced to curve her hands round his wide shoulders to rise on tiptoe so that he could hear her above the music.

Indifferent to the watchers around them, Sebasten linked his other arm round her slender, trembling length as well, fierce satisfaction firming his expressive mouth as he felt the tiny little responsive quivers of her body against his. 'It doesn't matter. You're going to be mine...'

And with that far-reaching assurance, retaining an arm at the base of her spine, Sebasten turned her round and headed her up the wrought-iron staircase.

You're going to be mine. Men didn't as a rule address such comments to Lizzie and normally such an arrogant assumption would simply have made her giggle. She got on well with men but few seemed to see her as a likely object of desire and her male friends often treated her like a big sister. Perhaps it was because she towered over most of them, was usually more blunt than subtle and never coy and was invariably the first to offer a shoulder to cry on. Until Connor, her relationships had been low-key, more friendly than anything else, drifting to a halt without any great grief on either side. Until Connor, she had not known what it was to feel ripped apart with inadequacy, pain and humiliation. Sebasten—and she had already forgotten his surname—was just what her squashed ego needed most, Lizzie told herself fiercely.

He took her up to the VIP room, the privilege of only a chosen few, and her conviction that he owned the club increased as she spread a bemused glance over the opulence of the luxurious leather sofas, the soft, expensive carpet and the private bar in the corner.

'We can hear ourselves think up here,' Sebasten pointed out with perfect truth.

Lizzie stared at him, for the first time appreciating that his more formal mode of dress had picked him out as much as his looks and height. His superb grey suit had the subtle sheen of silk and the tailored perfection of designer-cut elegance.

'Do you own this place?' she asked.

'No.' Sebasten glanced at her in surprise.

'Then who are you that you get so much attention here?' Lizzie enquired helplessly.

'You don't know?' Amusement slashed Sebasten's lean, bronzed features, for not being recognised and known for who and what he was was a novel experience for him. 'I'm a businessman.'

'I don't read the business sections of the newspapers,' Lizzie confided with palpable discomfiture.

'Why should you?'

Lizzie coloured. 'I don't want you thinking I'm an airhead.'

A tough, self-made man, her father had refused to let her take any interest in the family construction firm. As a teenager she had told him that she wanted to study for a business degree so that she could come and work for him and Maurice Denton had hurt her by laughing out loud at the idea. But then, that he had done well enough in the world to maintain his daughter as a lady of leisure had *once* been a source of considerable pride to him.

'I think you're beautiful...especially when you blush and all your freckles merge,' Sebasten mocked.

'Stop it...' Lizzie groaned, covering her hot face with spread hands in reproach.

He lifted a glass from the bar counter and she lowered one hand to grasp it, green eyes wide with fascination on his lean, strong face. Did he *really* think she was beautiful?

She so much wanted to believe he was sincere, for she was more used to being told she was great fun and a good sport. Her fingers tightened round the tumbler and she drank even though her head was already swimming.

'Very beautiful and *very* quiet,' Sebasten pronounced.

'Guys like talking about themselves…I'm a good listener,' Lizzie quipped. 'So what was the most exciting event of your week?'

Sleek black lashes lowered to partially screen his shimmering dark eyes. 'Something someone said to me after a funeral.'

Lizzie's soft lips parted in surprise and then sealed again.

'Connor Morgan's funeral…' Sebasten let the announcement hang there and watched her tense and lose her warm colour with quiet approval. He was no fan of coldhearted women and her obvious sensitivity pleased him. 'Did you know him?'

Lizzie's tummy muscles were tight as a drum but she kept her head high and muttered unevenly. 'I'm afraid that I never got to know him very well…'

It *was* true: she had barely scratched the surface of Connor's true nature, had been content to accept the surface show of the younger man's extrovert personality, had never once dreamt that he might lie to her and cheat on her without an ounce of remorse.

'Neither did I…' Sebasten's dark, deep drawl sent an odd chill down her spine.

'Let's not talk about it…' Taut with guilty anxiety over the near-lie she had told, Lizzie wondered if he was aware of the rumours and if he would have approached her had he known of her previous connection with Connor.

Aware he ought to be probing for some first-hand information on the voluptuous little blonde who had ditched his half-brother, Sebasten studied Lizzie's taut profile. However, his attention roamed of its own seeming volition down over her long, elegant neck to the tiny pulse beating out her tension beneath her collarbone and from there to the delicate curve of her breasts. By that point, his concentration had been engulfed by more libidinous promptings. Below the fine fabric, her nipples were taut and prominent as ripe berries and the dull, heavy ache at Sebasten's groin intensified with sudden savage force. Without hesitation, he swept the glass from her grasp and reached for her.

As she was sprung with a vengeance from her introspection, Lizzie's bemused gaze clashed with his and the scorching heat of his appraisal. She trembled, her body racing without warning to a breathless high of tension. Excitement, naked excitement flared through her, filling her with surprise and confusion. Dry-mouthed, pulses jumping, knees shaking, she felt his hand slide from her spine to the fuller curve of her behind and splay there to pull her close. She shivered in contact with the lean, tight hardness of his muscular thighs, every inch of her own flesh suddenly so sensitive she was bewildered, embarrassed, *shocked*.

'This feels good...' Sebasten husked, revelling in the way she couldn't hide her response to him. He could feel every little quiver assailing her, recognise the hoarseness of the breath she snatched in, read the bright luminosity of her dilated pupils and the full enticement of her parted lips.

'I hardly know you.' Lizzie was talking to herself more than she was talking to him. But that attempt to reinstate her usual caution didn't work. Being that close to him felt like perching at the very top of a rollercoaster a nanosecond before the breathtaking thrill of sudden descent and she was incapable of denying herself the seductive promise of that experience.

'I'll teach you to know me...' Sebasten framed with thickened emphasis, the smouldering glitter of his pagan golden eyes fixed to her with laser force. 'I'll teach you everything you need to know.'

'I like to go slow…'

'I like to go fast,' Sebasten imparted without hesitation, letting a lean brown hand rise to stroke through a long silken strand of her amber-coloured hair before moving to trace the tremulous line of her mouth with a confident fingertip. 'So fast I'll leave you breathless and hungry for more.'

Mesmerised, her very lips tingling from his light touch, Lizzie couldn't think straight. He might have been talking a foreign language, for right at that instant her leaping hormones were doing all of her thinking for her. She just wanted him to kiss her. In fact, she was so desperate to have that wide, sensual mouth on hers that she had to clench her hands to prevent herself from reaching for him first and, since she had never felt anything quite like that shameless craving before, it felt as unreal as a dream.

But when his mouth found hers, teased at her tender lips with a series of sensual little nips and tantalising expertise, no dream had ever lit such a powder-keg of response in Lizzie. Suddenly she was pushing forward into the hard, muscular contours of his powerful frame, hands flying up to link round his neck to steady her wobbling knees and from deep in her own throat a tiny moaning, pleading sound emerged as frustration at his teasing built to an unbearable degree.

He reacted then with a hungry, satisfying urgency that pierced her quivering length with the efficacy of a burning arrow thudding into a willing target. Suddenly he gave her exactly what she had wanted without even knowing it. As he drove her lips apart in a devastating assault of erotic intensity, her very skin-cell seemed to spontaneously combust in the whoosh of passion that shockwaved through her. Her own excitement was as intoxicating as a drug and all the more dangerous because raw excitement in a man's arms was new to her.

'*Theos mou,*' Sebasten groaned as he lifted his arrogant dark head. 'You're blowing me away…'

Bereft of his mouth on hers, Lizzie blinked in confusion. Only then conscious of the urgent tightness of her nipples and the pulsing ache between her thighs, she was surprised by the painful effect of both sensations. Her body didn't feel like her own any more. Her body was sending out frantic signals that the only place it was happy was up against *him*.

Sebasten flipped her round, curved her back to him again and let his hands glance over the pointed invitation of her sweet breasts, feeling her jerk and shiver and gasp as though she was in the eye of a storm. He eyed the nearest sofa. He didn't want to wait. He wanted her here, now, fast and hard to ease the nagging throb of his aroused sex. Sleazy, his mind told him while his defiant and fertile imagination threw up various explicit scenarios that threatened that conviction. No, he preferred to take her home to his own bed, where he could take his time, and he already knew once wouldn't be enough.

On fire from sensation, Lizzie broke free of him and dragged in a great gulp of oxygen. It was an effort to walk in a straight line to the table where he had set her drink. Lifting it with a shaking hand, she tipped it to her swollen lips, needing to occupy herself while she came to terms with the amazing feelings gripping her. She wanted to know everything about him from the minute he was born. She wanted to know him as nobody else had ever known him and a crazy singing happiness filled her when she looked back at him over the rim of her glass.

'I've never felt like this before,' she whispered with an edgy laugh that screened her discomfiture.

'I don't want to hear about how it felt with anyone else.' Burning golden eyes slammed into hers and he extended a commanding hand. 'Let's go...'

Lizzie moved and let him engulf her fingers in his. 'Are you always this bossy?'

'Where did you get that idea?' Sebasten purred like a very large and amused jungle cat because she had just leapt to do as he asked without even thinking about it. But then women always did. In his entire adult life, Sebasten had never met a woman who was *not* eager to please him.

He swept her back down the stairs, past a welter of curious eyes and on towards the exit. Her nerves were jumping like electrified beans. She relived the bold caress of his sure hands over her breasts and her cheeks flooded with hot self-conscious colour. Not the sort of familiarity she normally allowed. What was she doing with him? Where on earth was he taking her? *He* thought she was beautiful. *He* wanted to be with her, she reminded herself with feverish determination. Nobody else did, not her father, who had cut her out of his life, not a single one of her friends.

On the wet pavement outside, a uniformed chauffeur extended an umbrella for their protection and hurried to open the door of a long, opulent silver limousine. Lizzie was impressed and she got in, refused to think about what she was doing and turned to look at Sebasten again. The dizzy sense of rightness that had engulfed her only minutes earlier returned. 'Where were you born?' she heard herself ask.

In the act of tugging her close, Sebasten grinned at what struck him as an essentially feminine and pointless question. 'On an island the size of a postage stamp in the Aegean Sea…and you?'

'In Devon,' she confided, heart skipping a beat over that incredible smile of his. 'My parents moved to London when I was a baby.'

'How fascinating,' Sebasten teased, lacing his fingers into her hair and kissing her. She drowned in the scent and the taste of him, head falling back on her shoulders as his tongue darted in an erotic sweep between her lips and made her gasp with helpless pleasure.

At some point, they left the limo, climbed steps, traversed a low-lit echoing hall, but true awareness only returned to Lizzie when she swayed giddily on the sweeping

staircase she found herself on. His hands shot out to steady
her. 'Are you OK?'

'These stupid shoes...' Lizzie condemned in mortification and she kicked off her spike-heeled sandals where she
stood as though her unsteady gait had been caused by
them.

'How much have you had to drink?' Sebasten enquired
with lethal timing, a dark frown-line forming between his
ebony brows.

'Hardly anything,' Lizzie told him breathlessly while
making a conscious effort not to slur her words. She was
taut as a bowstring, suddenly terrified of receiving yet another rejection to add to the many she had already withstood.

As he received that assurance Sebasten's tension evap-
orated and he swept her on into a massive, opulent room
rejoicing in a very large and imposing bed. She was jolted
by the sight of the bed and a rather belated stab of dismay
made her question her own behaviour. She barely knew
Sebasten and she was still a virgin. But then she had never
been tempted until she met Connor and she had expected
him to become her first lover. As the degrading memory
of finding her boyfriend and her stepmother in bed together
engulfed Lizzie afresh, she rebelled against her own moral
conditioning. After all, hadn't her old-fashioned principles
let her down badly when it came to men? A more experienced woman would have been suspicious of Connor's
lack of lusty intent.

Eyes flaring like emerald-green stars on that bitter acknowledgement, Lizzie spun round and feasted her attention on Sebasten. He was gorgeous and tonight he was
hers, *all* hers, absolutely nobody else's. She had never met
anyone like him before. He was so focused, so sure of
himself that he drew her like a magnet and the heat of his
appreciative appraisal warmed her like the sun after weeks
of endless rain.

Lizzie tilted her head back, glossy marmalade hair tumbling back from her slanted cheekbones. 'You can kiss me again,' she informed him.

With an appreciative laugh, Sebasten claimed her parted lips in a long, drugging kiss that rocked her on her feet. Lifting her up into his arms with easy strength, he brought her down onto his bed. What was it about her that made her seem so different to other women? One minute she was quiet and mysterious, the next tossing an open challenge, glorious green eyes telegraphing pure invitation.

Lizzie surfaced from the mindless spell of her own response and stared up at him. 'Are you as good at everything else as you are at kissing?'

Sebasten tossed his jacket on a chair, enjoying the wide, wondering look in her face as she watched him. 'What do you think?'

That she could barely breathe when those shimmering dark golden eyes rested on her and her mouth ran dry as a bone when he unbuttoned his shirt. From his broad shoulders to his powerful, hair-roughened pectorals and flat, taut abdomen, he was all sleek, bronzed skin and rippling muscles.

'That you're very sexy,' Lizzie confided helplessly.

'We match…' Sebasten strolled lithe as a hunting animal and barefoot towards the bed.

'Do we?' Her heart hammered behind her ribs. She felt like an infatuated teenager confronted without warning by her idol: butterflies in her tummy, brain empty, teeth almost chattering with nerves. Every lingering strand of caution was urging her to acknowledge her mistake and take flight but those prudent promptings fell into abeyance at the same instant as Sebasten rested shimmering dark golden eyes of appreciation on her.

'Ne…'

'No?' Lizzie was confused.

'Ne…is Greek for yes.' Sebasten came down on the side of the bed with a smile that lit up his lean, strong face and melted her.

'You're Greek?'

'Ten out of ten,' Sebasten gathered her close and threaded lazy hands through her tumbling mane. 'I *love* the colour of your hair...but I still don't know your surname.'

In the expectant silence, Lizzie tensed. Fearful of his reaction were he to recognise the name of Denton, she heard herself quote her late mother's maiden name. 'Bewford.'

'Now I can't lose you again,' Sebasten asserted.

'Would it matter if you did?' Heart racing so fast now that she could barely speak and keep her voice level, Lizzie curved an uncertain hand round his arm.

'Absolutely, *pethi mou*.' Sebasten reflected that he might even make it to the three-month mark with her, a milestone he had yet to share with any woman. Unsettled by that uninvited and odd thought, he kissed her again.

He made love to her mouth with devastating virtuosity, plundering the tender interior she opened to him. Lizzie pressed forward, unsteady hands linking round his neck, fingers uncoiling to rise and sink into the depths of his luxuriant black hair. It was sweeter and wilder and more intense than anything she had ever known. He bent her back over his arm so that her bright hair trailed across the pillows and let his lips seek out the tiny pulse going crazy beneath her collarbone.

Lizzie quivered in surprise and what little grip she had left on reality vanished. When he then located the tender pulse spot below her ear, her body thrummed into a burst of life so that not one part of her was capable of staying still. She was not even conscious of the deft unsnapping of the clasps on her halter top, only of the air grazing her distended nipples and cooling the swollen sensitivity of her flesh. He eased off her stretchy skirt to leave her clad in only a pair of white lace panties.

'You're perfect,' Sebasten groaned, cupping the ivory-pale rose-tipped mounds he had unveiled with possessive hands, easing her back against the pillows to direct his attention to the tender tips straining for his attention.

Capturing a throbbing peak between his lips, he flicked it with his tongue and she moaned out loud at the surge of tormenting sensation that made her tense and tremble and jerk beneath his ministrations. Nothing before had ever felt so good that it almost hurt and she was lost in the shocking intensity of her own response. She was breathing in fast little pants, aware of her body as she had never been before, feeling the charged readiness of wild anticipation, the crazed race of her own pounding heartbeat, the damp heat pulsing between her thighs.

'Talk to me…' Sebasten urged.

'I…can't find…my voice,' Lizzie tried to say after a bemused hesitation in which she had to struggle just to force her brain to think again. Even to her own ears, the words emerged sounding indistinguishable and slurred.

Sebasten stilled and, scanning her dismayed face, he removed his hands from her. 'You're drunk…'

As that harsh judgement came out of nowhere at her, Lizzie flinched. Bracing herself on one awkward hand, she sat up. His lean, powerful face was taut, stunning golden eyes betraying angry distaste.

'I'm—'

'Out of your skull on booze…*not* my style!' Sebasten incised, springing upright to his full intimidating height.

Dragged with little warning from the breathtaking hold of unbelievable passion, Lizzie found herself in need of a ready tongue. But there was nothing ready about her tongue when her brain was in a haze of confusion. 'Not your style?' she echoed.

It was a terrible strain for her to try to enunciate each word with clarity. She reeled off the bed in an abrupt movement, suddenly feeling horribly naked and under attack.

As he watched her stagger as she attempted to stay vertical Sebasten's wide, sensual mouth clenched even harder, his whole body in the fierce grip of painful frustration while he questioned how he could possibly have failed to register the state she was in. 'The consent issue,' he breathed with icy restraint. 'No way would I even consider bedding a woman too inebriated to know what she is doing!'

Her toes catching in her discarded skirt where it lay, Lizzie tipped forward and only just managed to throw out her hands to break her own fall. As she went down with a crash, punctuated by a startled expletive from Sebasten, she just slumped on the soft, deep carpet.

With a mighty effort of will, Lizzie lifted her swimming head again and focused on Sebasten's bare brown feet. Even his toes were beautiful, she thought dimly as she tried to come up with something to say in a situation that had already gone far beyond embarrassment. 'Do you think…do you think you could sober me up before we continue?' she muttered hopefully.

CHAPTER THREE

SEBASTEN surveyed Lizzie with thunderous incredulity and then he wondered what he *was* going to do with her.

After all, he was responsible for her, wasn't he? He had pressed more alcohol on her when she must already have had enough and he had brought her into his home. In the condition she was in, he could hardly stuff her into a taxi or ask his chauffeur to cope with her and, since he too had had several drinks, he could not drive her anywhere.

In the tense silence which would have agonised Lizzie had she been sober, she surveyed his carpet fibres and then looked up. Sebasten was down on one knee, contemplating her with an expression of fierce frustration.

'I could just sleep here on the floor,' Lizzie proffered, striving to be helpful.

Sebasten collided with huge green eyes.

The beginnings of an irreverent grin pulled at her full, reddened mouth because she was suffering from a dreadful urge to succumb to uncontrollable giggles. 'You see...I don't think I can get up...can't feel my legs.'

Sebasten experienced a sudden near-overwhelming desire to shake her until he could force some sense back into her head. Had she no idea how much at risk she could be in a stranger's house? Or of how dangerous it was for a woman to drink so much that she could neither exercise caution nor defend herself? The very idea of her behaving in such a way with another man filled him with dark, deep anger.

'Do you make a habit of this kind of behaviour?' he demanded rawly.

As she was assailed by that gritty tone, all desire to

giggle was squashed at the source. 'No…you're the first…sorry,' Lizzie slurred, sinking back to the carpet again.

Vaulting to his feet, Sebasten strode over to the phone by the bed and lifted it to order a large pot of black coffee and sandwiches to be brought upstairs. Then he contemplated his victim with brooding intensity and his long, powerful legs carried him over to the windows. Depressing the locks, he thrust the French windows back to let in the cold night air.

As that chilly breeze touched her slender bare back, Lizzie gave a convulsive shiver. Sebasten surveyed her without remorse. He would sober her up and *then* have her conveyed home. Wrenching the top sheet from the bed, he flung it over her prone body and gathered her up with determination to carry her into the adjoining bathroom.

'Sleepy…' Lizzie mumbled.

'You need to wake up,' Sebasten informed her, settling her with some difficulty onto the seat in the spacious shower cubicle and hitting the buttons to switch on the water. Only as the water cascaded down did he appreciate that he hadn't removed the sheet. Then he no longer felt quite so comfortable with her semi-clad state.

As the water hit her, Lizzie opened bewildered and shaken eyes. 'No…don't want to be wet,' she framed weakly.

'Tough,' Sebasten told her, barring the exit in case she made a sudden leap for freedom.

Far from making a dive for it, in slow motion and wearing an only vaguely surprised expression, Lizzie slithered off the seat like a boneless doll into a heap on the floor of the cubicle.

'*Up!*' Sebasten urged in exasperation.

Lizzie curled up and closed her eyes, soothed now by the warm flooding flow of water. 'Sleepy,' she mumbled again. 'Night…night.'

Teeth gritted, Sebasten stepped into the shower to hit

the controls and turn the water cold. She uttered a satisfying yelp of surprise as the water went from warm and soothing to icy and tingling. However, Sebasten got so wet in his efforts to haul Lizzie's uncooperative body back up onto the seat, he ended up squatting down to hold her up and suffering beneath the same cold gush.

'C-cold!' Lizzie stammered.

'I'm freezing too!' Sebasten launched, shirt and trousers plastered to his big, powerful body as the same chill invaded him. He withstood the onslaught with masochistic acceptance. Served him bloody well right, he thought grimly. She was way too young and immature for him. What had got into him? Bringing her home had been a mistake and he had never sunk low enough to take advantage of a stupid woman.

'*Very*…cold,' Lizzie moaned.

'And you said you weren't an airhead,' Sebasten recalled out loud with a deep sense of injustice, watching her wet hair trail in the water, looking down at her miserable face which was now—aside of the odd streak of mascara—innocent of all cosmetic enhancement. She still had perfect skin and amazing eyes, he noted. But he could not credit that he was trapped in his own shower with a drunk woman. He didn't get into awkward situations like that.

'*Not*,' Lizzie pronounced with unexpected aggression, her chin tilting up.

A loud knock sounded on the door in the bedroom beyond. With a groan, Sebasten put her down but she slumped without his support. A vision of having to explain a drowned woman in his shower overtaking him, he switched off the water.

'Don't move…' he instructed Lizzie as he strode back to the bedroom, dripping every step of the way.

A faint flush over his hard cheekbones as the member of staff presenting the laden tray of coffee and sandwiches stared in open stupefaction at his drenched appearance,

Sebasten kicked the door shut again and set down the tray beside the bed.

When he returned to the bathroom, Lizzie was striving to crawl out of the shower on her hands and knees and being severely hampered by the trailing sopping sheet.

'Feeling a little livelier?' Sebasten quipped with dark satire.

'Feel…*a-awful*!' Lizzie stuttered through teeth chattering like castanets and she laid her head down and just sobbed in weakened rage. 'Hate you!'

She looked pathetic. Sebasten snatched up a big bath towel, crouched down to disentangle her from the sheet and wrapped her with care into the towel. Hauled up into a standing position, she fell against him like a skater on ice for the first time and he lifted her up and carried her through to the bedroom to settle her back on the bed. Keeping a cautious eye on her in case she fell off the bed too, he backed away to strip off his own wet clothing and pitch the sodden garments onto the bathroom floor.

It was like babysitting, he decided, his even white teeth gritting. Not that he had ever *done* any babysitting, for Sebasten was not in the habit of putting himself out for other people. But the comparison between his own erotic expectations earlier in the evening and reality was galling to a male who was accustomed to a life than ran with the smooth, controlled efficiency of an oiled machine.

'Close the windows…' Lizzie begged, deciding there and then as cold dragged her mind from its former fog that she had fallen live into the hands of a complete sadist.

'Yes, you're definitely waking up now.' Sheathed only in a pair of black designer jeans, Sebasten crossed the room to pull the French windows shut.

Lizzie blinked and then contrived to stare. The jeans fitted him as well as his own bronzed skin, accentuating his flat, muscular stomach, his narrow hips and long, hard thighs. Colouring, she looked away, sobered up enough already by the shock of that cold shower to cringe with mortification. Sebasten tugged her forward, tossed pillows behind her to prop her up and proceeded to pour the coffee.

'Don't feel like coffee—'

'You're drinking it,' Sebasten told her and he laid the tray of sandwiches down beside her. *'Eat.'*

'I'm not hungry,' she dared in an undertone.

'You need food to soak up the booze in your system,' Sebasten delivered with cutting emphasis.

Squirming with shame and embarrassment, Lizzie reached for a sandwich. 'I don't get drunk...I'm not like that...I just had a hideous day—'

'So you decided to give me a hideous evening,' Sebasten slotted in with ungenerous bite. 'Count your blessings—'

'What blessings?' Lizzie was fighting hard to hold back the surge of weak tears that that crack had spawned.

'You're safe and you're still all in one piece. If you'd picked the wrong guy to spring this stunt on, you might not have been,' Sebasten pointed out.

Chilled by what she recgonised as a fair assessment, Lizzie swallowed shakily and made herself bite into the sandwich. It was delicious. Indeed, she had not realised just how hungry she was until that moment. In silence, she sipped at the black coffee, wincing with every mouthful, for she liked milk in her coffee, and worked her way through the sandwiches.

Sebasten watched the sandwiches melt away and noted that for all her slenderness she had a very healthy appetite. 'When did you last eat?' he finally asked drily.

'Breakfast,' Lizzie worked out with a slight frown and that had just been a slice of toast. Lunch she hadn't touched because just beforehand her father had phoned to say that he was coming home specially to talk to her and her appetite had vanished. As for supper, well, Jen hadn't offered her anything but her first alcoholic drink of the evening.

'No wonder you ended up flat on your face on my carpet,' Sebasten delivered as he topped up the cup she had emptied.

Lizzie paled. 'Not the world's most forgiving person, are you?'

'No.' Sebasten made no bones about the fact. 'What did your "hideous" day encompass?'

Lizzie looped unsteady fingers through her fast-drying hair to push it back from her brow and muttered tightly. 'My father told me to move out and get a job. I was *very* upset—'

'At twenty-two years of age, you were still living at home and dependent on your family?' Sebasten demanded in surprise. 'Are you a student?'

Lizzie reddened. 'No. I left school at eighteen. My father didn't *want* me to work. He said he wanted me to have a good time!'

Sebasten scanned the delicate diamond pendant and bracelet she wore, conceding that they might well be real rather than the imitations he had assumed. Yet she didn't speak with those strangulated vowel sounds that he associated with the true English upper classes, which meant that she was most probably from a family with money but no social pedigree. He was wryly amused that Ingrid, who was obsessed by a need to pigeon-hole people by their birth and their bank balance, had taught him to distinguish the old moneyed élite from the *nouveau riche* in London society.

'And, *no*…having a good time did not cover my behaviour tonight!' Lizzie advanced in defensive completion. 'That was a one-off!'

'So you were *very* upset at the prospect of having to keep yourself,' Sebasten recapped with soft derision and innate suspicion that her apparent ignorance of who he was had been an act calculated to bring his guard down. 'Is that why you came home with me?'

Startled by that offensive question, Lizzie sucked in a sudden sharp breath. As the fog of alcohol released her brain, she had already absorbed enough of her surroundings to recognise that she was in the home of a male who inhabited a very much wealthier and more rarefied world than her own. She lifted her chin. 'No, to tell you the truth, now that I'm recovering my wits, I haven't the foggiest idea *why* I came home with you because I don't like you one little bit.'

A disconcerting smile flashed across Sebasten's dark, brooding features. Angry green eyes the colour of precious emeralds were hurling defiance at him and her spine was as rigid as that of a queen in a medieval portrait. Unfortunately for her, though, her tangled hair and the bath towel supplied a ridiculous frame for that attempt to put him in his place.

The instant that incredible smile lit up his lean, strong features, Lizzie's heartbeat went haywire and her mouth ran dry and she knew exactly why she had come home with him. If he kept his smart mouth closed, he was just about irresistible.

'You're angry that you made a fool of yourself,' Sebasten retaliated without hesitation. 'But I may have done you a big favour—'

Hot colour burned in Lizzie's cheeks. 'You call throwing the windows wide and torturing me in a cold shower doing me a *favour*?'

'Yes…if the memory of that treatment stops you drinking that much again in the wrong company.'

Unused to a woman fighting with him, Sebasten savoured the sheer frustrated rage in her expressive face and his body hardened again in sudden urgent response. He wanted to flatten her back onto his bed and remind her of how irrelevant liking or anything else was when he touched her. His own reawakened desire startled him. Then her tangled torrent of hair was drying to gleam with rich gold and copper lights and that exotic and passionate face of hers still kept drawing him back. The intimate recollection of her lush little breasts and that lithe, slender body of hers shaking with hunger beneath his own was all the additional stimuli required to increase Sebasten's level of arousal to one of supreme discomfort.

In the midst of swallowing the sting of that further comment destined to humble her, Lizzie felt the burn of Sebasten's stunning dark golden eyes on her and what she had been about to say in an effort to save face died on her tongue. Stiffening, she shifted forward onto the edge of the bed. Suddenly aware of the high-voltage tension that had entered the atmosphere, she felt too jittery to handle her discomfiture and she settled her feet down onto the carpet.

'It's time I went home,' she announced but she hesitated, afraid that the awful dizziness might return the instant she tried to stand up.

'Where is home?'

'No place right now,' Lizzie admitted after a dismayed pause to appreciate the threatening reality. 'I still have to find somewhere to live. Right now my luggage is parked at a friend's place but I can't stay there.'

Sebasten watched her stand up like a newborn baby animal afraid to test her long slim legs and then breathe in slow and deep. She plotted a passage to the bathroom and vanished from view. Closing the door, she caught her own reflection in a mirror and groaned out loud, lifting a trembling hand to her messy hair. Any pretence towards presentability was long gone, she reflected painfully. It was little wonder Sebasten had been sprawled in an armchair at a distance, talking down to her as if he were a very superior being.

And she guessed he *was*, she conceded, snatching up a comb from the counter of a built-in unit to begin disentangling her hair. He could have thrown her back out on the street. He could have taken advantage of her…well, not really, she decided, reckoning that Sebasten would prefer a live, moving woman to one showing all the animation of a corpse. And he *had* prevented her from making a very big mistake! Why didn't she just admit that to herself? Her life was in a terrible mess and she shouldn't even have been looking at Sebasten, never mind behaving like a tramp and coming home with him. She ought to be really grateful that nothing much had happened between them…

Only she *wasn't*. Tears stung the back of Lizzie's eyes and she blinked them back with stubborn determination. The ghastly truth was that she still found Sebasten incredibly attractive and she had blown it. Really blown her chances with him. There was nothing fanciable or appealing about a woman who had to be dumped in a shower to be brought out of a drunken collapse, naturally he was disgusted with her. But she was much angrier with herself than he could possibly have been. She had never been so attracted to any guy and she was convinced that alcohol had had very little to do with her extraordinary reaction to him. Why had she had to meet the most gorgeous guy of her life on the one night that she made a total, inexcusable ass of herself?

Wishing that she had thought to reclaim her clothing before she entered the bathroom and embarrassed to death as stray memories of her wanton behaviour broke free of her subconscious to torment her, Lizzie crept back into the bedroom.

Dawn was beginning to finger light through the heavy curtains. She had hoped that Sebasten would have fallen asleep or taken himself tactfully off somewhere else to allow her a fast and silent exit but no such luck was hers.

Sebasten was watching the television business news but the instant the door opened he vaulted upright and studied her. Still wrapped in the towel, hair brushed back from her scrubbed-clean face, she looked even more beautiful to Sebasten than she had looked earlier. Even pale, she had a fresh, natural appeal that pulled him against his own volition.

'You might as well sleep in one of my guest rooms for

what's left of the night,' Sebasten surprised himself by suggesting.

'Thanks…but I'd better be going.' Strained eyes centred on him in a look so brief he would have missed it had he not been watching her like a hawk. 'I've taken up enough of your time.'

His mouth quirked. She sounded like a little girl who had attended a very bad party but was determined to leave saying all that was polite. He watched her stoop in harried movements to snatch up her clothes and shoes, mortification merging her freckles with a hot pink overlay of colour. Her inability to conceal her embarrassment was oddly touching.

'How sober are you?' Sebasten prompted lazily, eyes flaring to smouldering gold as her lush mouth opened and the tip of her tongue snaked out in a nervous flicker to moisten her full lower lip. Hunger, fierce and primitive as a knife at his groin, burned through him.

'Totally wised up…' Lizzie tried hard to smile, acknowledging her own foolishness.

'Then *stay* with me…' Sebasten murmured thickly.

Thrown by that renewed invitation, Lizzie gazed across the room, green eyes full of surprise and confusion. 'But—'

'Of course there *are* conditions,' Sebasten warned, smooth as silk. 'With your eyes closed, you have to be able to touch the tip of your nose with one finger and you only get one chance.'

An involuntary laugh escaped Lizzie as she looked back at him. Still clad only in the jeans, he was drop-dead gorgeous: all sleek, bronzed, hair-roughened skin, lean muscle and masculinity. Even the five o'clock shadow now roughening his strong jawline only added to his sheer impact. Feeling just then that it would be more sensible to close her eyes and deny herself the pleasure of staring at him as though he had just dropped down from heaven for a visit, Lizzie strove to play the game and performed the exercise even though at that point she had every intention of leaving.

'Then you have to open your eyes again and walk in a straight line to the door,' Sebasten instructed.

Growing amusement gripping her, Lizzie set out for the door.

'Full marks,' Sebasten quipped.

Lizzie spun round. 'You've got to do it *too*.'

Disconcerted, Sebasten raised a brow in scornful dismissal of that challenge.

'You take yourself very seriously.' Lizzie watched him with keen intensity because it was one of the most important things she had learnt about him. 'You don't even like me to suggest that you might be anything less than totally in control.'

'I'm a man. That's normal,' Sebasten drawled.

Not to Lizzie, it wasn't. She was used to younger men who were more relaxed about their image and the differences between the sexes but she could see that Sebasten inhabited another category altogether. The strong, brooding, macho type unlikely to spill his guts no matter how tough the going got. Not her type at all, she told herself in urgent consolation.

Sebasten strode in a direct line to the door but only because where she was was where he wanted to be at that instant. 'Satisfied?'

'Yes…we are two sober people…and I need to go and get dressed.' Breathless at finding herself that close to him again, Lizzie coloured, heartbeat thumping at what felt like the base of her throat.

'I'll only take it all off again,' Sebasten threatened in a dark, deep undertone of warning that sent a tingle of delicious threat down her taut spine.

'Walking in a straight line to the door when you asked was just my effort to lighten the atmosphere,' Lizzie shared awkwardly.

'While every lingering look you give me tells me how

much you still want me,' Sebasten delivered without an instant of hesitation.

'You've got some ego!' Lizzie condemned in disconcertion.

'*Earned*…like my reputation,' Sebasten slotted in, closing his lean, sure hands to her slender waist to tilt her forward. 'We'll conduct an experiment—'

'No…*no* experiments,' Lizzie cut in on a higher pitch of nervous stress. 'I don't *do* stuff like this, Sebasten. I don't have one-night stands. I don't sleep with guys I've only just met…in fact, I haven't got much experience at all and you'd probably find the business news more riveting—'

Sebasten recognised one of the qualities that had drawn him to her but which he had failed to identify: a certain degree of innocence. Fired by the rare event of being challenged to persuade a woman into his bed, he focused his legendary negotiating skills on Lizzie. 'I'm riveted by *you*,' Sebasten incised with decisive conviction. 'Right from the first moment I saw you at the club.'

'Stop kidding me…' Skin warming, Lizzie connected with his stunning golden eyes and trembled, wanting to believe, her battered self-esteem hungry for that reassurance. That close to him, it was difficult to breathe and the warm, clean male scent of his skin flared her nostrils with a familiarity that tugged at her every sense. She wanted to lean into him, crush the tender tips of her swollen breasts into the hard wall of his chest, feel that wide, sexy mouth ravish her own again.

'I'm not kidding. One look and I was hooked.' Sebasten gazed down at her from below the dense fringe of his black lashes and just smiled and that was the moment she was lost, that was the moment when any pretence of self-control ran aground on the sheer strength of her response to him. Her pulses racing, Lizzie felt the megawatt burn of that smile blaze through her and she angled into him in a helpless movement. When his mouth came down on hers again, the heat of that sensual assault was pure, addictive temptation.

In the midst of that kiss, Sebasten carried her back to the bed and peeled away the towel. He cupped her breasts, bent his arrogant dark head over the pale pink distended peaks and used his knowing mouth and his even more knowing hands to give her pleasure.

'Are you protected?' he asked.

'Yes…' She had started taking contraceptive pills a month after she had begun dating Connor but she crushed that unwelcome association back out of her mind again, the bitterness that had haunted her in recent weeks set behind her. A fresh start, a new and more productive life, Sebasten. She was more than ready for those challenges when Sebasten was giving her the impression that *he* felt much the same way that *she* did.

As he slid off the bed in one fluid movement to dispense with his jeans, her cheeks reddened and she turned her head away while wicked but self-conscious anticipation licked along her every nerve-ending.

He came down beside her again and she let her hands rise up over his powerful torso. She had never really wanted to explore a man before but she could not resist her need to touch him. Her fingers roved from the satin-smooth hardness of his shoulders to graze through the short black whorls of hair hazing his pectorals to the warm tautness of his stomach, feeling his muscles flex in response.

'Don't stop there, *pethi mou*,' Sebasten husked.

Lizzie got more daring, let her fingers follow the intriguing furrow of silky black hair over his stomach and discovered the male power of him with a jolt of mingled dismay and curiosity. He was smooth and hard but there was definitely too much of him.

'*This way*,' Sebasten murmured with concealed amusement, initially startled by her clumsiness and then adapting to teach her what he liked. It was a lesson he had never had cause to give before but it sent his desire for her surging even higher.

That intimate exploration made Lizzie feel all hot and quivery and she pressed her thighs together on the disturbing ache stirring at the very heart of her. When he teased at her swollen lower lip before letting his tongue delve into the tender interior of her mouth in a darting foray that imitated a far more elemental possession she trembled against his lean, strong body, feverish hot craving gripping her.

His breathing fractured, Sebasten dragged his mouth from hers to gaze down at her with fiery golden eyes. 'I don't think I've ever been so hot for a woman as I am for you.'

He pulled her to him and his expert hands traced the beaded sensitivity of her breasts. She couldn't stay still any more. Tiny little tremors were racking her. Her breath was rasping into her dry throat, pulses thrumming, heart pounding. At the apex of her legs he traced the moist, needy secret of her femininity and she moaned out loud, couldn't help herself. The pleasure was dark and deep and terrifyingly intense. He controlled her and she didn't care; she just didn't want him to stop. The bitter-sweet torment of sensation sizzled through every fibre of her writhing body with increasing intensity until she was on the edge of a desperation as new to her as intimacy.

'I need you…*now*,' Sebasten growled.

Rising over her, he tipped her up with strong hands and came down over her. She barely had time to learn the feeling of his urgent demand for entrance before he plunged his throbbing shaft into her slick heat and groaned with an earthy pleasure at the tightness of his welcome.

The momentary stab of unexpected pain made Lizzie jerk and cry out but the passionate urgency controlling her allowed no competition. Too much in the grip of the feverish need he had induced, she gave him a blank look when he stilled in questioning acknowledgement of that cry. Her whole body craved him with a force of hungry excitement that nothing could have haltered and she arched up to him in frantic encouragement until he succumbed to that invitation and ground his body into hers again, sheathing himself fully and sending another shockwave of incredible desire through her. His pagan rhythm drove her to the edge of ecstasy and then flung her over the wild, breathtaking peak before the glorious, peaceful aftermath of fulfilment claimed her. As he reached his own shuddering release, she wrapped her arms round him tight.

'Sublime,' Sebasten muttered hoarsely in Greek and then he rolled back and hauled her over him to study her flushed and shaken face, the unguarded softness and warmth in her green eyes as she looked back at him. He pushed his fingers into her tumbling hair and tugged her back down to him so that he could kiss her again. 'I think we're going to do this again and again…and again.'

'Hmm…' Lizzie was more mesmerised by him than ever now. She scanned his lean, strong face and let her fingertips roam from his shoulder to curl into his tousled black hair instead. His features were *so* masculine: all taut angles from the clean slant of his high cheekbones to the proud jut of his nose and the blue-shadowed roughness of his hard jawline. His stunning gaze gleamed lazy gold beneath the semi-screening sweep of his spiky lashes. She just wanted to smile and smile and smile like an idiot.

She had been a virgin, he was *sure* of it, Sebasten thought, but he wasn't quite sure enough to broach the issue. He recalled her clueless approach to making love to him and amusement filled him. A split-second later the renewed ache of desire prompted him to kiss her again and it was the last even semi-serious thought he had for some hours.

Lizzie wakened with a start, feeling horribly queasy.

Sebasten was asleep. Sliding as quietly as she could from the bed, she fled to the bathroom, where nature took its course with punishing efficiency. Humbly grateful that Sebasten had not witnessed the final reward for her own foolishness, Lizzie got into the shower and used his shampoo to wash her hair. Even the already familiar smell of his shampoo turned her inside-out with intense longing. She felt weak, frighteningly vulnerable and yet crazily happy too. Yet hadn't she honestly believed that she was in love with Connor? What did that say about her? Connor had never lowered her to the level of sniffing shampoo bottles. Connor had never turned her brain to mush with one smile, never made her feel *scared*...

Yes, she *was* scared, Lizzie acknowledged as she made use of the hair-dryer and surveyed her own hot, guilty face in the mirror. She was in wholly uncharted territory and she was scared that Sebasten would just think of her as a one-night stand and would not want to see her again. Wouldn't that be just what she deserved? After all, how much respect could he have for a woman who just fell into his arms the very first night she met him? A woman, moreover, whom he had had to sober up first from the most disgusting state of inebriation. Shame and confusion enveloped Lizzie as she recalled how she had behaved *and* how he had reacted: angry and sardonic but essentially decent in that he had looked after her.

In the bedroom next door, Sebasten asked himself if he ought to be sympathetic towards her being ill and decided that support or sympathy might only encourage her to repeat the offence in the future. No, he definitely didn't want to risk that. He might be almost convinced that she was not an habitual drunk but it was his nature to be cautious with women. So they had a future? He could not remember ever thinking that with a woman before and it really spooked him.

Springing out of bed, Sebasten lifted the phone and ordered breakfast and might well have made it into the bathroom to join her in the shower had he not stood on her tiny handbag where it had been abandoned on the floor the night before.

With a muttered curse as he wondered whether he had broken anything inside it, he swept it up and the contents fell out because the zipper hadn't been closed. Reaching for the items, he thrust them back into the bag and in that rather impatient handling her driver's licence slipped out of her purse. He studied her photograph with a smile and was in the act of putting it back when he saw the name.

Liza Denton.

What the hell was Lizzie doing with another woman's driving licence in her possession? Sebasten stilled with a dark frown until he looked back at the photograph and the truth exploded on him with all the efficacy of an earthquake beneath his feet. Lizzie was usually short for Elizabeth but mightn't it also be a diminutive for Liza? In thunderous disbelief, he recalled the club manager pointing out the small blonde on the dance floor the night before. It dawned on him then that the man might well have been pointing at Lizzie instead, for the two women had been standing together.

In a rare state of shock, Sebasten stared back down at the photo. Lizzie was Liza Denton, the vindictive, man-hungry tramp who had driven his own kid brother to self-destruction. Sebasten shuddered. Not only had Lizzie pretended to have only the most tenuous acquaintance with Connor, but she had also outright *lied* by giving him a false surname! Her awareness of the notoriety of her own name and her deliberate concealment of her true identity was, in his opinion, absolute proof of her guilt.

Lizzie Denton was a class act too, Sebasten acknowledged as he threw on clothes at speed, ferocious rage rising in direct proportion to the raw distaste now slicing through him. That he should have *slept* with the woman whom poor Connor had loved to distraction! That he himself should then have been taken in to the extent of believing her to be a virgin! Sebasten snatched in a harsh breath.

On top of that first shattering discovery the conviction that the judgement and intelligence that he prided himself on should have fallen victim to a clever act was even more galling. Of course, it had been an act calculated to impress! So calculating a woman would be well aware that, for a male as cynical and bone-deep Greek as he was, a pretence of sexual innocence had immense pulling power. For he *had* liked that idea, hadn't he? The idea that he was the *first* to make her feel like that? The first to stamp that look of shellshocked admiration on her lovely face?

And why had she done it? Well, hadn't she told him that herself? And very prettily too with tears glistening in her big green eyes. Her adoring daddy had pulled the plug on her credit line and she had to be desperate to find a rich and generous boyfriend to keep her in the style to which she was accustomed, sooner than accept the hard grind of the daily employment that others less fortunate took for granted as their lot in life. Then Lizzie Denton had not bargained on dealing with Connor's big brother, had she?

In the fiery space of a moment, Sebasten knew exactly what he was about to do and little of his usual caution was in evidence. He would play her silly games until she was wholly in his power and then when she least expected it he would dump her as publicly as she had dumped Connor. He would repay lies with lies, hurt with hurt and pain with pain. It might not be the towering revenge he had quite envisaged but then why should her entire family suffer for her sins when it was evident that her father had already repudiated his daughter in disgust? It would be a much more *personal* act of vengeance…

With a chilling smile hardening his handsome mouth, Sebasten knocked on the bathroom door, cast it open only a few inches, for he did not yet trust himself to look her in the eye without betraying the sheer rage still powering him. 'I'll see you for breakfast downstairs…'

CHAPTER FOUR

HAVING stolen one of Sebasten's shirts from a unit in the dressing room to cover her halter top, Lizzie descended the stairs in hopeful search of a dining room. She was a bag of nerves, her heart banging against her ribs.

Sebasten had not even waited for her to emerge from the bathroom and he had sounded so cold and distant when he had said that he would see her downstairs. After the night they had shared, it was not the way she had naïvely expected him to greet her and now she was wondering in stricken embarrassment if he was eager just to get her out of his house. Perhaps only some refined form of good breeding had urged him to offer breakfast at noon.

*One look and I was hooked…*wasn't that what Sebasten had told her the night before? For an instant, she hugged that recollection to her and straightened her taut shoulders. But then maybe that had only been the sort of thing the average male said when things got as far as the bedroom. When she had no other man to compare him with, how would she know? Furthermore, he *wasn't* the average male, was he? Lizzie stole an uneasy glance at the oil paintings and the magnificent antique collector's cabinet in the huge hall. Everywhere she looked, she was seeing further signs of the kind of stratospheric wealth that could be rather intimidating.

A manservant appeared from the rear of the hall and opened a door into a formal dining-room, where Sebasten was seated at the end of a long polished dining-table. Colliding unwarily with veiled dark golden eyes as he rose upright with the kind of exquisite manners that she was unused to meeting with, she felt a tide of colour warm her

pale complexion, and broke straight into nervous speech.
'I pinched one of your shirts. I hope you don't mind.'

'I should have sent out for some clothes for you,'
Sebasten countered, throwing her into a bewildered loop
with that assurance and then the unsettling suspicion that
he brought a different woman home at least three times a
week. 'My apologies.'

As the unfamiliar intimate ache at the heart of her tense
body reminded her of just how passionate and demanding
a lover Sebasten was, Lizzie dragged her tense gaze from
his in awful embarrassment and sank down fast into a seat.

Sebasten was very tempted to give her a round of ap-
plause for her performance. The blushing show of discomfiture was presumably aimed at convincing him that she
had never before spent a night with a man and faced him
the next morning.

'I have an apartment you can use,' he murmured evenly.

Startled by that sudden offer of accommodation, Lizzie
glanced up. 'Oh…I wouldn't dream of it.'

'I can't bear to think of you being homeless,' Sebasten
quipped.

'Well, I won't be after I've found somewhere of my
own, which I intend to do today,' Lizzie hastened to add,
grateful for the distraction of the food being presented to
her by the manservant.

'It's not that easy to find decent accommodation in
London,' Sebasten countered.

'I'll manage. Thousands do and so will I. In fact, I'm
looking forward to proving to my father that I can look
after myself,' Lizzie admitted. 'I did offer to leave home
after Dad remarried but he wouldn't hear of it. He had a
self-contained flat built in the stable block at the back of
the house for me.'

Settling back in his antique rosewood carver chair,
Sebasten cradled his black coffee in one lean brown hand
and surveyed her with a frown-line dividing his level ebony brows. 'I can't understand why the indulgent father

you describe should suddenly go to the other extreme and practically *throw* you out of your home.'

Visibly, Lizzie lost colour and after some hesitation said, 'Dad thinks he's spoilt me rotten—'

'Did he?'

'Yes,' Lizzie confided ruefully. 'And I have to be honest and admit that I *loved* being spoilt.'

'Any man would feel privileged to offer you the same treatment,' Sebasten drawled, smooth as glass.

Lizzie laughed out loud. 'Stop sending me up!' she urged.

Grudging appreciation flared in Sebasten's veiled gaze. She was clever, he conceded. She had not snatched at the apartment he had mentioned and was determined to demonstrate an appealing acceptance of her reduced circumstances. 'So what *are* your plans?'

Lizzie thought of the number of bills she had to settle and almost flinched. Before leaving home she had trotted up the sum total of her liabilities, and she was well aware that without her father's generous allowance only the sale of her jewellery and her car would enable her to keep her head above water on a much smaller budget. However, she had no intention of startling him with those uncomfortable realities.

'Somewhere to live is my first priority and then a job.'

It was evident that he had made use of another bathroom while she hogged his own. His black hair was still damp, his strong jawline clean shaven and she couldn't stop staring at him. Inherent strength and command were etched in his devastatingly attractive features and, regardless of the little sleep he had enjoyed, no shadows marked the clarity of his dark golden eyes. Even in his mood of cool reserve that increased her own apprehension as to how he now saw her, she was fascinated by him.

'On the career front, try the Select Recruitment agency.' Sebasten not only had a controlling interest in the business but also used it to recruit all his own personal staff. 'I've heard that they're good.'

'They would need to be,' Lizzie remarked with a wry twist of her lush mouth. 'I have no references, only basic qualifications and very little work experience to offer.'

'I'm sure you'll manage to package your classy appearance and lively personality as the ultimate in saleable commodities. It all comes down to presentation. Concentrate on what you can do and *not* what you can't,' Sebasten advised.

Grateful for his advice and the indirect compliment, Lizzie nibbled at a delicious calorie-laden croissant spread with honey and sipped at her tea. Did he want to see her again? She thought *not*. As her hand trembled, the cup she held shook and she set it back on the saucer in haste. Don't be such a baby, she urged herself furiously, willing back the stinging moisture at the backs of her eyes. Indeed she might console herself with the reflection that what had been so special for her had probably been *equally* special for him in that she could not credit that he made a regular habit of sharing cold showers with a drunk.

As the grandfather clock in the corner struck the hour, Sebasten rose to his feet again with a sigh. 'I'm afraid I have a lunch engagement I can't break at my club but my chauffeur will drive you back to wherever you're staying. Please don't feel that you have to hurry your meal.'

'It's OK…I've finished anyway.' With a fixed and valiant smile, Lizzie extracted herself from behind the table with uncool speed and walked back out to the hall ahead of him, her hand so tight on her bag that her knuckles showed white. No, she wasn't very good at this morning-after-the-night-before lark and possibly it was a lesson she had needed. Never, ever again would she drink like that, never, ever again would she let a squashed ego persuade her to jump into bed with a guy she had just met.

Possibly being awkward and gauche came naturally to her, Sebasten reflected in surprise, raising a brow at her headlong surge from his dining room. She was behaving like one of his dogs did when he uttered a verbal rebuke: as though he had taken a stick to her. He was pretty certain that Connor had not exercised similar power over her and grim amusement lit his keen gaze.

'I might as well give you a lift,' he proffered equably, determined to drag out her discomfiture for as long as he could. 'What's the address?'

Ensconced in the opulent limousine while Sebasten made a phone call and talked in Greek, Lizzie was just counting the minutes until she could escape his company. She watched him spread the long, shapely fingers of one lean, bronzed hand to stress some point that he was making and her tummy flipped at the helpless recollection of how he had made her feel in his bed: driven, possessed, wild, ecstatic. All unfamiliar emotions on her terms and mortifying and painful to acknowledge in the aftermath of an intimacy that was not to be repeated.

Having made arrangements to have her followed every place she went, Sebasten flipped open a business magazine out of sheer badness until the limo drew up outside the smart block of flats where she was staying. Only as she leapt onto the pavement like a chicken fleeing the fox did he lean forward and say, 'I'll call you...'

Lizzie blinked and her long, naturally dark lashes swept up on her surprised eyes as she nodded, staring back at him while his chaffeur hovered. 'You don't have my number,' she suddenly pointed out and before he could be put to the trouble of asking for it, she gave him the number of her mobile phone.

When Lizzie finally sped from view, slim shoulders now thrown back, marmalade hair blowing back like a banner in the breeze and long, perfect legs flashing beneath her short skirt, Sebasten was recovering from the new experience of being told that *nobody* had a photographic memory for numbers and then directed to punch hers straight into his phone so that he didn't forget it because she wouldn't be at her current address much longer.

Without a doubt, he was now recognising what might have drawn Connor in so deep, Connor, who had had strong protective instincts for the vulnerable: that jolly-schoolgirlish bluntness she practised, that complete seeming lack of a cool front, that seductive, what-you-see-is-what-you-get attitude she specialised in. And it was novel, different, but it *was* indisputably a pose designed to charm and mislead, Sebasten decided in contemptuous and angry dismissal.

Did I really make him put my number straight into his phone? Lizzie asked herself in shock as she stepped into the lift. Oh, well, he already knew how keen she was and at least that way she deprived herself of the time-wasting comfort of wondering if he had just forgotten her number when he didn't call. And he wouldn't call, she was convinced he wouldn't call, because he had been polite but essentially aloof.

At no stage had he made the smallest move to touch her in any way and yet he was a very hot-blooded guy, the sort of male who expressed intimacy with contact. Indeed, looking back to the instant of their first meeting the night before, she was challenged to recall a moment when he had not automatically maintained some kind of actual physical contact with her. Yet in spite of that, when she joined him for breakfast he had been as remote as the Andes around her. Then why had he offered her the use of an apartment? Maybe such a proposition was no big deal to a male who might well deal in property, maybe it had even been his way of saying thanks for a sexually uninhibited night with a total tart. After all, weren't all single men supposed to secretly crave a tart in the bedroom?

As Jen answered the doorbell, Lizzie was pale as death from the effects of that last humiliating thought.

'You have a visitor,' Jen informed her in a disgruntled

tone, her pretty face stiff with annoyance. 'Your step-mother has been plonked in my sitting room since twelve, waiting for you to put in an appearance.'

At that announcement and the tone of it, Lizzie stiffened in dismay. What on earth was Felicity playing at? All that needed to be said had been said and it was still a punishment for her to even look at her stepmother. And did Jen, who had invited her to stay in the first place, really have to be so sour?

'Look, I'll get changed and get rid of her and then I'll be out of here just as fast as I can get my cases back into my car,' Lizzie promised, hurrying down to the bedroom, refusing to subject herself to the further embarrassment of greeting Felicity in an outfit that spelt out the demeaning truth that she had not slept anywhere near her own ward-robe the night before.

Clad in tailored cream cotton chinos and a pink cash-mere cardigan, Lizzie walked into Jen's sitting room ten minutes later. Felicity spun round from the window, a tiny brunette, barely five feet one inch tall with a gorgeous figure and a tiny waist that Lizzie noted in surprise was still not showing the slightest hint that she had to be almost four months pregnant. Her classic, beautiful face was dominated by enormous violet-blue eyes. Predictably, those eyes were already welling with tears and Lizzie's teeth gritted.

'When your father told me what he had done, I was devastated for you!' Felicity gushed with a shake in her breathless little-girl voice. 'I felt *so* guilty that I had to come straight over here and—'

'Check out that I would continue to keep quiet about you and my former boyfriend?' Lizzie slotted in with distaste, for the brunette's shallow insincerity grated on her. 'I gave you my word that I wouldn't talk but it's not something I want to keep on discussing with you.'

'But how on earth will you cope without your allow-ance?' Felicity demanded. 'I've been thinking...*I* could help you out. Maurice is very generous and I'm sure he wouldn't notice.'

Hush money, Lizzie found herself thinking in total revulsion. 'I'll manage.'

Felicity gave her a veiled assessing look that was a poor match for her tremulous mouth and glistening eyes. 'You've never been out there on your own and you don't know how hard it can be. If only I didn't have our baby's future to think of, I *swear* I would have told your father the truth.'

The truth? And which version would that be? Lizzie thought back to the conflicting stories that Felicity and Connor had both hurled at her in the aftermath of her inopportune visit to the cottage which had become their secret love-nest. Her stepmother's priorities had been brutally obvious. Felicity had had no intention of surrendering her comfortable lifestyle and adoring older husband to set up home with an impecunious lover. As he had listened to the brunette lie in her teeth about their affair and accuse him of trying to wreck her *happy* marriage, Connor's jaw had dropped, his disbelief palpable. When her stepmother had followed up that with the announcement that she was pregnant, Lizzie's shock had been equal to Connor's devastated response.

Dredging herself back from her disturbing recollections of that day, Lizzie was so uncomfortable that she could no longer stand to look at the other woman. 'Dad will come round in his own good time. And with Connor gone, you have nothing to worry about.'

'That's a wicked thing to say…' Felicity condemned tearfully.

But deserved, Lizzie reflected. It would be a very long time before she forgot the flash of relief that she had seen in the brunette's face when she had first learnt that Connor had died in a car crash. But then what was the point of striving to awaken a conscience that Felicity did not have?

The brunette had few deep emotions that did not relate to herself.

As soon as Felicity had gone, Lizzie got stuck into repacking her luggage. Jen appeared in the bedroom doorway and remarked. 'If it's any consolation, we were all eaten alive with raging envy when you landed Sebasten Contaxis last night...'

Encountering the sizzling curiosity in the pert blonde's gaze, Lizzie coloured and concentrated on gathering up the cosmetics she had left out on the dressing-table.

'Mind you,' Jen continued, 'I hear he's a real bastard with women...lifts them, *lays* them, then forgets about them. But then who could blame him? He's a young, drop-dead gorgeous billionaire. Women are just arm candy to a guy like that and of course he's happy to overdose on the treats.'

Even as a chill of dismay ran over Lizzie that Sebasten's reputation should be that bad with her sex, she angled up her chin. 'So?'

'When you get dumped, everyone will crow because you weren't entitled to get him in the first place. He dates supermodels...and let's face it, you're hardly in that category. It's my bet that, once he gets wind of all the nasty rumours there have been about you and Connor, you'll never hear from him again!'

'Thank you for the warning.' In one move, Lizzie carted two cases out to the hall in her eagerness to vacate the blonde's apartment. 'But I wasn't actually planning on *dating* Sebasten. I was just using him for a one-night stand.'

Twenty minutes later, Lizzie climbed into her Mercedes four-wheel-drive and the startled look on Jen's spiteful face travelled with her. It had been a cheap, tasteless response but it had made Lizzie feel just a little better. So where did she go now that she was truly homeless and friendless? Well, she had better try to sell her little horde of jewellery first to get some cash so that she could pay upfront for accommodation.

*   *   *

One week later, Lizzie dealt her new home a somewhat shaken appraisal. Six nights in an overpriced bed and breakfast joint and then *this*...

Her bedsit was a dump and, as far as she could see, a dump with no secret pretensions to be transformed into a miraculous palace. But then neither her car nor her jewellery had sold for anything like the amount that she had naïvely hoped, and until she had actually trudged round the rental agencies and checked the newspapers she had had no idea just how much it actually cost to rent an apartment. Any solo apartment, even the *tiniest* was way beyond her budget and, since she had been reluctant to share with total strangers, a bedsit had been her only immediate option.

But on the bright side, she had an interview the next day. When she got a job she would make new friends and then possibly find somewhere more inspiring to live, and in the meantime life was what you made of it, Lizzie told herself sternly. She would buy herself a bucket of cheap paint and obliterate the dingy drabness of the walls rather than sit around drowning in self-pity!

Sebasten had *not* called. Well, had she really expected him to? An aching wave of regret flooded Lizzie. It was so hard for her to forget the sense of connection that she had felt with him, that crazy feeling that something magical was in the air. Indeed she had slept with her mobile phone right beside her every night. However, the something magical had only been her own stupid fantasy, she conceded, angry that she still hadn't managed to get him out of her mind. After all, if what Jen had said about Sebasten's reputation was true, she had had a narrow escape from getting her heart broken and stomped on. In any case, how could she possibly have explained why she had lied and given him a false surname?

Reading his security chief's efficient daily bulletins on Lizzie's fast-disintegrating life of ease and affluence had supplied the major part of Sebasten's entertainment throughout the past week.

Lizzie had been conned into flogging her six-month-old-low mileage Mercedes for half of its worth and then ripped off in much the same way when it came to parting with her diamonds. Having run a credit check on her, Sebasten had appreciated the necessity for such immediate financial retrenchments and could only admire her cunning refusal to snatch at his offer of an apartment. Evidently, Lizzie was set on impressing on him the belief that she was not a gold-digger or a free-loader. Now in possession of both her Merc and her jewellery and having paid very much more for both than she had received for either, Sebasten was ready to make his next move.

When her mobile phone sang out its musical call, Lizzie was standing on top of three suitcases, striving to get the paint roller to do what it was supposed to do as easily as it did in the diagram on the back of the pack. It had been so long since her phone rang that it took her a second or two to recognise the sound for what it was. With a strangled yelp, she made a sudden leap off the precarious mound of cases, the roller spattering daffodil-yellow paint in all directions as she snatched up her phone with all the desperation of a drowning woman.

'Sebasten…' Sebasten murmured.

Lizzie pulled a face, suddenly wishing she knew at least three Sebastens and could ask which he was. At the same time, she rolled her eyes heavenward, closed them and uttered a silent heartfelt prayer of thanks. He had called…he had called…he had *called*!

'Hi…' she answered, low-key, watching paint drip down from the ceiling, knowing that she had overloaded the roller and now wrecked her only set of sheets into the bargain and not caring, truly not caring. Her brain was in a blissful fog. She couldn't think straight.

'You'd better start by giving me your address,' Sebasten

told her before he could forget that he wasn't supposed to know it already.

Lizzie rattled it off at speed.

'Dinner tonight?' Sebasten enquired.

Her brain peeped out from behind the romantic fog and winced at that last-minute invitation. Breathing in deep and slow, she dragged her pride out of the hiding place where it was eager to stay. 'Sorry I can't make it tonight.'

'Try...' Sebasten suggested, a wave of instant irritation gripping him. 'I'll be abroad next week.'

Lizzie paled at that additional information and then surveyed the devastation of the room which she had only begun to paint. 'I really *can't*. I'm in the middle of trying to decorate my bedsit—'

'I've had some novel excuses in my time but—'

'If I leave it now, I'll never finish it...are you any good at decorating?' Lizzie asked off the top of her head, so keen was she to break into that far from reassuring response of his.

'Never wielded a paintbrush in my life and no ambition to either,' Sebasten drawled in a derisive tone of incredulity, thinking that she was taking the I'm-so-poor façade way too far for good taste. Decorating? *Him?* She just had to be joking!

Wishing she had kept her mouth shut, Lizzie felt her cheeks burning. Of course, a male of his meteoric wealth wasn't about to rush over and help out. But it was hardly her fault that she wasn't available at such very short notice, and for all she knew he had only called because some other woman was otherwise engaged. 'Oh, well, looks like I'm on my own. To be frank, it's not a lot of fun. I'd better go...I've got paint dripping everywhere but where it should be. Maybe see you around...thanks for calling. Bye!'

Before she could weaken and betray her anguished regret, she finished the call. Maybe see you around? Lizzie flinched. Some chance! Her fashionable nights out on the town in the top clubs and restaurants were at an end.

In outraged disbelief, Sebasten registered that she had cut him off. Who the bloody hell did Lizzie Denton think she was? When the shock of that unfamiliar treatment had receded, a hard smile began to curve his wide, sensual mouth. She was trying to play hard to get to wind him up and increase his interest. He phoned his secretary and told her to find him a decorator willing to work that night.

By six that evening, Lizzie was whacked and on the brink of tears of frustration. Practically everything she possessed including herself was covered with paint and the first layer on the ceiling and two of the walls had dried all streaky and horrible. When a knock sounded on the door, she thrust paint-spattered fingers through her tumbled hair and tugged open the door.

Sebasten stood there like a glorious vision lifted straight from some glossy society-magazine page. His casual dark blue designer suit screamed class and expense and accentuated his height and well-built, muscular frame. A flock of butterflies broke loose in her tummy and her heartbeat hit the Richter scale while she hovered, staring at him in surprise.

'What are you wearing?' Sebasten enquired, brilliant golden eyes raking over what looked very like a leotard but his true concentration absorbed by the lithe perfection of the female body delineated by the thin, tight fabric. Instantaneous lust ripped through him and smouldering fury at his lack of control over his own libido followed in its wake.

'Exercise gear…I didn't have anything else suitable.' She was unsurprised that he was staring: she knew she had to look a total fright with no make-up on. 'I'd have been better doing it naked!' she quipped tautly, her mind a total blank while she tried to work out what he was doing on her doorstep.

Naked; now there was an idea… Sebasten stopped that

forbidden thought dead in its tracks but lust had a more tenacious hold still on his taut length.

'I've brought a decorating crew…and we're going out to dinner,' he informed her, scanning the chaos of the room and the horrendous state of the walls with elevated brows of wonderment, certain that should he have taken the notion he could have done a far more efficient job. 'Grab some clothes. We'll stop off at my place and you can get changed there, leaving the crew to get stuck in.'

'You've brought…*decorators*?' Lizzie was still staring at him with very wide green eyes, striving to absorb his announcement that he had drummed up decorators to finish her room for her. She was stunned but even more stunned by the manner in which he just *dropped* that astonishing announcement on her. As if it was the most natural thing in the world that he should hire decorators so that she could be free to join him for dinner. This, she registered, was a male who never took no for an answer, who put his own wishes first, who was willing to move proverbial mountains if it got him what he wanted.

'Why not?' Sebasten turned his devastating smile on her and, in spite of her discomfiture at what he had done and what it revealed about his character, her heart sat up and begged and sang at that smile. 'You did say painting wasn't a lot of fun.'

'And I'm not exactly brilliant at it,' Lizzie muttered, head in a whirl while she reminded herself that it was also a compliment that he should go to such extravagant lengths just to spend time with her. He might not be willing to wield a paintbrush for her benefit but he was certainly no sleeper in the practicality stakes.

'*So?*'

Aware of his impatience and even while telling herself that she ought not to let herself react to that or be influenced by his macho methods into giving instant agreement, Lizzie found herself digging into the wardrobe and drawing out a raincoat to pull on over her leotard. 'I'm a complete mess,' she pointed out anxiously, grabbing up a bag and banging back into the wardrobe and several drawers to remove garments.

'You'll clean up to perfection,' Sebasten asserted, planting a lean hand to her spine to hustle her out of the room.

'Are you always this ruthless about getting your own way?' Lizzie asked breathlessly after she had passed her keys over to the businesslike-looking decorators waiting by their van on the street below and had warned them that she had bought rubbish paint.

'Always,' Sebasten confirmed without hesitation, lean, powerful face serious. 'I work hard. I play hard. And I didn't want to wait another week before I saw you again, *pethi mou.*'

Clutching her raincoat round her, Lizzie tried to keep her feet mentally on the ground but her imagination was already soaring to dizzy heights. Presumably he had been really, really busy all week but couldn't he at least have called to chat even if he hadn't had the time to see her sooner? Squashing that unwelcome reflection, she discovered that she couldn't wait to tell him about the highlight of her week.

'I've got an interview for a job tomorrow afternoon,' she told him with considerable pride.

'Where?'

'CI...it's a big City Company,' Lizzie advanced with a grin.

Sebasten veiled his amused gaze with dense black lashes. Select Recruitment had come up trumps on his request and even faster than they had promised, for the agency had not yet come back to him to confirm that she had paid them a visit. CI was *his* company and the fact that she hadn't even registered yet that CI stood for Contaxis International did not say a lot about the amount of homework she had done in advance of the interview. Or was she just pretending and did she know darned well that it was his company?

'Of course, it's only a temporary position where I fill in for other people on holiday and stuff but I gather that if I do OK it *could* become permanent,' Lizzie continued.

'You sound as if you're just gasping to work,' Sebasten mocked, knowing that there was no possibility on earth that the position would become permanent as it had been dreamt up at his bidding and styled to deliver the maximum pain for the minimum gain. He couldn't wait to see her application form and discover how many lies she had put in print.

'Of course I am…I'm skint!' Lizzie exclaimed before she could think better of it.

As she encountered Sebasten's enquiring frown, a wave of colour ran up from her throat to mantle her cheekbones. 'Well, don't tell me you're surprised,' she said ruefully. 'I'm not living in a lousy bedsit so far out of the city centre so I'll need to rise at dawn to get into work just for the good of my health!'

'I can't understand why you didn't accept the apartment I mentioned…but then the offer remains open,' Sebasten delivered.

'Thanks…but I've got to learn to look after myself. I was so annoyed when I screwed up the painting project,' Lizzie confided truthfully. 'I didn't appreciate that it wasn't as easy as it looked and I *hate* giving up on anything! I should have stayed and watched those guys work and learned how to do it for myself.'

'Let's not go overboard.' Sebasten reckoned that the number of fresh challenges awaiting her at CI would prove quite sufficient to occupy her in the coming weeks.

An hour and a half later, Lizzie scanned her appearance in the mirror in the opulent guest room she had been shown into in Sebasten's beautiful town house. She had enjoyed freshening up in a power shower, for it was slowly sinking in on her that a thousand things that she had once taken for granted were luxuries she might never get to experience again. Her dress was leaf-green with a cut-away back and a favourite, but in the rush to leave her bedsit she had forgotten all her cosmetics.

As she descended the stairs she thought about how much she had appreciated not being shown into *his* bedroom as if how the evening might end was already accepted fact. It wasn't. She had her interview tomorrow and she wanted to be wide awake for it and, furthermore, she suspected that it might be unwise to fall into Sebasten's arms too soon, at least not before she had got to know him better.

When Sebasten watched her descend his magnificent staircase, he stilled.

Feeling self-conscious, Lizzie pulled a comic face. 'Want to change your mind about being seen out with me? I forgot my make-up.'

'You have fabulous skin and I like the natural look.'

'All men say that because they think anything artificial is somehow a deception being practised on them but very few of them are actually *wowed* by the natural look if they get it!' Lizzie laughed.

Their arrival at the latest fashionable eaterie caused a perceptible stir of turning heads and inquisitive eyes. Afraid of seeing any familiar faces and meeting with an antagonistic look which would take all the gloss off her evening, Lizzie looked neither to her right nor her left and stared into stricken space on the couple of occasions that Sebasten broke his stride to acknowledge someone, for she was terrified that he might try to introduce her using the false name she had given him. Mercifully he did not but she saw that there was no escaping the unpleasant fact that she would *have* to admit to lying and give him an acceptable explanation for her behaviour.

As soon as the first course was ordered, Lizzie breathed in deep and dived straight in before she could lose her nerve. 'I have a confession to make,' she asserted, biting at her lower lip, green eyes discomfited. 'And I don't think you're going to like me very much after I've told you. My surname isn't Bewford, it's—'

'Denton,' Sebasten filled in, congratulating her mentally on her timing, for few men would contemplate causing a scene or staging a confrontation in a restaurant where, whether she had noticed it or not, they were the cynosure of all eyes. Yes, he had definitely found a foe worthy of his mettle.

Taken aback, Lizzie stared at him. 'You already *know* who I really am?'

Never one to tell an untruth without good reason, Sebasten explained that he had seen her driving licence that morning a week ago.

Lizzie paled. 'Oh, my goodness, what must you have thought of me?' she gasped in shamed embarrassment, re-calling his failure to await her emergence from his bath-room and his subsequent coolness on parting from her and now seeing both events in a much more presentable light. 'I'm really sorry...and I'm just *amazed* that you wanted to see me again after I'd told a stupid lie like that!'

'As to what I thought...I assumed you would explain when the time was right and that you must have a very good reason for giving me a false name. As to not seeing you again...' Brilliant dark golden eyes rested with keen appreciation on her lovely, flushed face, absorbing the anx-iety stamped into every line of it with satisfaction. 'I'm not sure that was ever an option. We shared an incredible night of passion and I want to be with you.'

Relief and shy pleasure mingled in Lizzie's strained ap-praisal and she decided that she owed him the fullest pos-sible explanation in return for his forebearance. 'I was—er—sort of *involved*,' she stressed with reluctance, 'with Connor Morgan up until a few days before he died. I don't know whether you're aware of the rumours—'

Sort of involved? Sebasten wanted to laugh out loud in derision at that grotesque understatement. The troubled plea for understanding in her beautiful eyes was an even more effective ploy. Lounging back in his seat as the head waiter appeared to refresh their wine glasses, Sebasten endeavoured to ape the role of a sympathetic audience. 'I had heard the suicide story but I also understand that he never made any such threat and that he left no note either.'

Relieved to hear him acknowledge those facts, Lizzie clutched her wine glass like a life belt and then put it down again, her hands too restless to stay still. 'If I tell you the whole truth, will you promise me that you won't repeat it to anybody?'

His contempt climbing at that evident request not to carry the lies she was about to tell to any other source, who might fast disprove her story, Sebasten nodded in confirmation but then murmured. 'Connor called you Liz, not Lizzie…didn't he?'

'That was typical Connor,' Lizzie sighed. 'He had an ex called Lizzie and he always insisted on calling me Liza.'

'So tell me about him…' Sebasten encouraged.

'I first met Connor just over three months ago. I liked him; well, we all did. He was the life and soul of every event.' Lizzie frowned as she strove to pick her words, for inexperienced she might be, but she knew that discussing her previous relationship with the new man in her life might not be the wisest idea. 'I suppose I developed quite a crush on him but I never expected anything to come of it. When he grabbed me one night at a party and kissed me and then asked me out, I was surprised because I didn't think I was his type…and as it turned out, I *wasn't*.'

'Meaning?'

'That four days before he died, I discovered that Connor had been using me as cover for his steamy affair with a married woman.' Lizzie winced as Sebasten's intent appraisal narrowed in disbelief. 'I know it doesn't sound very credible because Connor always seemed to be such an upfront guy but it's the truth. I found them together and nobody could have been more shocked than I was.'

'Who was she?' Sebasten enquired, impressed by her creativeness in a tight spot, for her tale was a positive masterpiece of ingenuity. In one fell swoop, she sought to turn herself from a heartless little shrew into a cruelly deceived victim and Connor into a cheat and a liar. His anger on his late half-brother's behalf smouldered beneath the deceptive calm of his appraisal.

'I can't tell you that. It wouldn't be fair because I gave my word to the woman involved that I wouldn't. She was very distressed and she regretted the whole thing and she broke off with him. All I can tell you is that he believed he was crazy about her but I think that for *her* it was just a little fling because she was bored with her marriage.'

'I'm curious. Tell me her name,' Sebasten prompted afresh, ready to put her through hoops for daring to tell him such nonsensical lies.

Her persistence made her squirm with obvious discomfiture. 'I'm sorry, I can't. Anyway, now it's all over and behind me, I can see that Connor really just treated me like a casual girlfriend he saw a couple of times a week…we didn't sleep together or anything like that,' she muttered, her voice dwindling in volume, but she had wanted to let him know that last fact. 'But it was still a very hurtful experience for me and I didn't like him very much for making such an ass of me.'

'How could you?' Sebasten encouraged, smoother than silk.

'It wasn't until I drove down to Brighton to try and pay my respects to his mother that I realised that *I* was getting the blame for his death. People just assumed that he'd got drunk and crashed his car because I had ditched him,' Lizzie shared heavily.

Ingrid had not admitted that Lizzie had made a personal visit to her home, Sebasten recalled, hating the way women always told you what they wanted you to hear rather than simply dispensing all the facts. 'What happened?'

'Mrs Morgan said some awful things to me…I can forgive that,' Lizzie stated but she still paled at the recollection of Ingrid Morgan's vicious verbal attack on her. 'I mean, she was just beside herself with grief and naturally

Connor hadn't admitted to his own mother that he was carrying on with someone else's wife. She said that if I tried to go to the funeral she'd have me thrown out of the church!'

'So you've been getting the blame for events that had nothing to do with you. That's *appalling*,' Sebasten commented with harsh emphasis.

'It's also why all my friends have dropped me and my father showed me the front door,' Lizzie confided, grateful for the anger she recognised in both the taut set of his hard bone-structure and the rough edge to his dark, deep drawl, for she believed it was on her behalf.

'Surely you could have confided in your own father?'

Lizzie tensed, averted her gaze and thought fast. 'No—er—he knows the woman concerned and I don't think I could rely on him to keep it quiet.'

'I'm astonished *and* impressed by your generosity towards a woman who doesn't deserve your protection at the cost of your own good name,' Sebasten drawled softly.

'Wrecking her marriage wouldn't bring Connor back and I'm sure she's learned her lesson.' Lizzie studied her main course without appetite, certain that she had just put paid to any sparkle in the evening with her long-winded and awkward explanation.

Sebasten reached across the table and covered her clenched fingers where they rested with his own. 'Relax…I understand why you lied to me. You were seriously *scared* that after one extraordinary night with you I might make a real nuisance of myself.'

After a bemused pause at that teasing and laughable assertion, Lizzie glanced up, amusement having driven the apprehension from her green eyes, and she grinned in helpless appreciation, for with one mocking comment he had dissolved her tension and concluded the subject. He was clever, subtle, always focused. Meeting his dark golden gorgeous eyes, she felt dizzy even though she was sitting down.

They had a slight dispute outside the restaurant when Sebasten assumed she was coming home with him.

'Where else are you going to go?' he demanded with stark impatience. 'The decorators aren't finished yet!'

'How do you know that? By mental telepathy?'

'I only needed to take one look at the havoc you wreaked with a paintbrush. They'll be lucky to finish by dawn!' Sebasten forecast.

'Call them and check.' Lizzie smothered a large yawn with a hurried hand, for she was becoming very sleepy.

'I can't…don't know how to reach them. Even if they had finished you couldn't sleep in a room full of paint fumes,' Sebasten spelt out, getting angrier by the second because the very last thing he had expected from her was an exaggerated pretence of *not* wanting to share his bed again, most particularly when *he* was determined not to repeat that intimacy. 'The bed I'm offering you for the night doesn't include me!'

'Oh…' Lizzie computed that surprising turn of events and gave him full marks for not acting on the supposition that her body was now his for the asking. 'That's fine, then. Thank you…thank you very much.'

Never had Sebasten snubbed a woman with so little satisfying effect. With an apologetic smile, Lizzie climbed into his limo, made not the smallest feline attempt to dissuade him from the rigours of a celibate night and then compounded her sins by falling asleep on him. He shook her awake outside his town house.

'Gosh, have I been asleep? How very boring for you,' she mumbled, stumbling out of the car and up the steps, heading for the stairs with blind determination but pausing to remove her shoes, which were pinching her toes. 'I'm almost asleep standing up. I shouldn't even have had *one* glass of wine over dinner.'

But for all her apparent sleepiness, Lizzie was thinking hard. She might have been pleased that he had no expectations of her, but when it dawned on her that she was

heading for his guest room and that he had still not even
attempted to kiss her she was no longer quite so content.
Telling him about Connor, it seemed, had been a horrible
mistake. It had turned him right off her.

On the landing her stockinged feet went skidding out
from under her on the polished 'floor and she fell with a
wallop and hit her knee a painful bash. 'What is it about
your wretched house?' she demanded, the pain hitting her
at a vulnerable moment and bringing a flood of tears to
her eyes. 'It's like…booby-trapped for my benefit!'

In instinctive concern, Sebasten crouched down beside
her. Tears were running down her face in rivulets and he
assumed she had really hurt herself. 'I'd better get an am-
bulance—'

'Don't be stupid…I only bumped it…I'm just being a
baby!' Lizzie wailed in mortification. 'I'm tired and it's
been a tough week, that's all.'

And when she cried, she really cried, Sebasten noted.
There were no delicate, ladylike sniffs, no limpid, brimming looks calculated to induce male guilt. She just put
her head down and sobbed like a child. She was miserable.
He *should* be happy about that. Lean, powerful face taut,
he snatched her up off the floor and into his arms. Rea-
soning that sticking her in a guest room alone with her
distress would not only seem odd but also suspicious behaviour for a male supposed to be interested in her, he
carried her into his room, where he deposited her on the
bed and backed off.

With a tremendous effort of will, Lizzie gulped into silence and squeezed open her swollen eyes. It was true that
she was very tired but it was her over-taxed emotions
which had brought on the crying jag. In the frame she was
in, she didn't think that she was capable of having a relationship with anybody. She missed her home, she missed
her father.

'I'm sorry you met me last week,' Lizzie confided

abruptly. 'You're never going to believe that I'm not normally like this.'

From the shadows outside the pool of light shed by the bedside lamps, Sebasten strolled forward. 'Have a bath. Get some sleep. You're exhausted.'

'Not very sexy... Exhaustion, I mean,' she muttered, plucking at the sheet with a nervous hand, peering out from under her extravagant torrent of hair, which shone with copper and gold lights.

'I'll be up later...I've got a couple of calls to make.'

'Kiss me goodnight,' Lizzie whispered on a breathless impulse before he reached the door.

Sebasten stopped dead and swung round, emanating tension. 'Surely, feeling so tired, you're not up for anything tonight?'

'So if there's no—er sex, you don't kiss either,' Lizzie gathered and nodded, although she was cut to the bone at his rejection.

'Don't be ridiculous!'

'You don't fancy me any more?' Lizzie was determined to get an answer.

Sebasten strode across the room, closed firm hands over her arms and hauled her up onto her knees on the mattress. She could have drowned in the pagan glitter of his splintering golden eyes. He brought his mouth plunging down on hers and it was like being pitched into a stormy sea without warning. Excitement shivered and pulsed through her in answer, heat and craving uniting at the thrumming heart of her body until she went limp in his hold, all woman, all invitation.

'I hope that answers that question,' Sebasten breathed thickly, dark colour accentuating his fabulous cheekbones as he let her sink back from him in sensual disarray.

Lizzie had a soak in his sunken bath, let the water go cold while she waited for him to join her. Then, ashamed of her own wanton longing, she took advantage of another one of his couple of hundred shirts and climbed into bed. That fiery, demanding kiss had soothed her though and she drifted off to sleep with a dreamy smile on her face…

CHAPTER FIVE

LIZZIE opened her eyes just when morning light was spilling through the bedroom and found Sebasten wide awake and staring down at her.

She didn't feel shy or awkward; she just felt happy that he was there. Indeed, so right and natural did it feel that she might have been waking up beside him for absolute years. But then had she been, she might have been just a little more cool at the effect of that all lean, bronzed, hair-roughened masculinity of his poised within inches of her. With a languorous stretch, she gazed up into the dark golden eyes subjecting her to an intense scrutiny and her heart fluttered like a frantic trapped bird inside her.

'Good morning,' she whispered with her irrepressible smile. 'You shouldn't stare. It wakes people up.'

Three brandies and a cold shower had failed to cool Sebasten's ravenous arousal and he had never been into celibacy. It was just sex, he reasoned, thought and integrity had nothing to do with it and denying himself was a pointless sacrifice when he had already enjoyed her.

He threaded caressing fingers through a shining strand of her amber hair and then knotted it round his fist to hold her fast, his stunning eyes semi-screened by his lush black lashes to feverish gold. 'Lust is keeping *me* awake, *pethi mou.*'

'Oh…' Breathing had already become a challenge for Lizzie.

'*And* you've been nicking my shirts again…there's a price to pay.' Long brown fingers flicked loose the topmost button and she quivered, melting like honey on a hot plate and mesmerised by his dark male beauty.

'Will I want to pay it?'

'I *know* you will,' Sebasten husked, releasing another button with tantalising slowness, watching her spine arch and push her pert little breasts up tight against the silk, delineating the straining pink buds already eager for his attention.

'How do you know?' Lizzie prompted unevenly, mortified by his absolute certainty of his welcome.

'Your exquisite body is screaming the message at me…' Sebasten parted the edges of the shirt with the care of a connoisseur and bent his arrogant dark head to graze his teeth over a pale pink swollen nipple.

Her entire body jackknifed up towards his, a low, moaning cry breaking from her lips.

With a groan, Sebasten lifted his head again. 'Different rules this time. You lie still…if you move or cry out, I stop.'

'S-sorry?' she stammered.

'You get too excited too fast.'

'That's wrong?' Lizzie had turned scarlet.

A shimmering smile flashed across Sebasten's lean, bronzed features. 'I want an excuse to torture you with sensual pleasure…*give* me it.'

A quiver of wild, wanton anticipation sizzled through Lizzie. 'I'll just lie back and—er—think of painting then—'

'It's going to be a lot more exciting than watching paint dry,' Sebasten promised with a husky laugh of amusement, scanning her expressive face.

And she found out that it *was* within minutes. The tension of struggling to stay still and silent no matter what he did electrified her with heat and desperate craving. He shaped her tender breasts, toyed with the throbbing peaks until every muscle in her shivering length was whip-taut and then switched his attentions to other places that she had never dreamt had even the tiniest erotic capability. But she soon found out otherwise. Sebasten ran his mouth down her spine and she was reduced to a jelly. He sucked her fingers and she was ready to flare up in flames, wild, helpless, terrified he might stop as he had threatened, turn off that wholly seductive, enslaving flow of endless exciting pleasure.

'You're doing really good,' Sebasten groaned and it was an effort to find the words in English as a telling shudder racked his big, powerful frame. The challenge he had set her from the pinnacle of his own bedroom supremacy was gnawing with increasing savagery and ego-zapping speed at his own self-control.

Lizzie gave him a smile old as Eve, leant up and ran the tip of her tongue in provocation and encouragement along his sensual lower lip and he growled and pushed her back against the pillows and drove his mouth down on hers with raw, hungry demand. Literal fireworks went off inside her. She was with him every step of the way, ecstatic at the change of pace that matched her own fevered longing and impatience.

'I want you...*now*!' Sebasten ground out hoarsely, hauling her under him with an incredible lack of cool when she had not the smallest intention of arguing.

And then he was there where she had *so* needed him to be, coursing into her and burying himself deep. Her climax was instant, shattering. Shorn of all control, she was thrown to a fierce peak and then she splintered into a million shellshocked pieces in an experience so intense she was left in a daze.

'You're a lost cause,' Sebasten bit out with a sudden laugh and then he kissed her, slow and tender, and her heart gave a wild spin as though it were a globe on a hanger.

'Sorry,' she muttered but that was the exact moment that she realised that she was in love, head over heels, fathoms-deep in love as she had never been before.

'Don't be...you're incredible in bed,' Sebasten assured

her, reminding himself that tomorrow was another day to
reinstate restraint before he took her to heaven and
back again.

Exactly a fortnight later, Lizzie experienced her first day
at work.

Her concentration was not all that might have been:
Sebasten was due back that afternoon from his *second* trip
abroad since she had met him. In the intervening weeks,
he had only managed to see her twice, once meeting her
for dinner when he was actually *en route* to the airport,
and on the second occasion taking her to the races to help
him entertain a group of foreign businessmen in his private
box. As neither event had entailed anything in the way of
privacy, Lizzie was counting the hours until she could see
him again and could indeed think of nothing else *but*
Sebasten.

True love, she recognised ruefully, had taken a long
time to hit her. What she had felt for Connor had just been
a practice run for the main event. Connor had damaged
her pride, her self-confidence and her blind faith in others
more than her heart. With Sebasten, she had discovered an
entire new layer of more tender feelings. She worried
about the incredible hours he seemed to work. She cherished every tiny thing she found out about him but
Sebasten could be stingier than Scrooge when it came to
talking about himself. His different moods fascinated her,
for the cool front he wore concealed a volatile tempera-
ment controlled by rigid self-discipline. He was full of
contradictions and complexities and every minute she
spent with him, even on the phone, plunged her deeper
into her obsession with him.

Even so, the poor start she contrived to make at CI on
her first day annoyed and frustrated her.

'A couple of little points,' Milly Sharpe, the office manager on the sixth floor, a whip-thin redhead in a navy business suit, advanced with compressed lips. 'Getting off at

the wrong tube station is not an acceptable excuse for being late. Please ensure that you arrive at the correct time tomorrow. Did you receive a copy of the CI dress code?'

Lizzie almost winced. 'Yes.'

'The code favours the darker colours, suits—longer skirts or trousers—and sensible shoes. The key word is *formal*, not casual.'

There was a pause while a speaking appraisal was angled over Lizzie's fashionable green skirt worn with a matching fitted top that sported *faux* fur at cuff and neckline and the very high sandals on her slender feet. Lizzie reddened and wondered if the woman honestly believed that she had the wherewithal to rush out and buy a complete new wardrobe. She had never bought dark colours, had never owned sensible shoes that were not of the walking-boot variety and her trouser collection consisted of jeans, chinos and pure silk beach wear.

'I would suggest that you also do something with your hair. It's a little too long to be left *safely* loose when you're working with office equipment.'

It was worse than being back at school, Lizzie thought in horror, waiting to be told to take off her earrings and removed her nail polish as well.

By the time Lizzie was shown to the switchboard and taken through a bewildering number of operations while various messages flashed up lightning-fast on the screen in front of her, sheer nervous tension had killed her ability to concentrate on the directions she was being given or remember them.

The hours that followed were a nightmare for her. She learnt that if she pressed the wrong button, she created havoc. She put calls through to lines that were engaged, cut people off in the middle of conversations, connected calls to the wrong extensions, lost others in an endless loop which saw them routed round the building and back to her again. The amount of abuse she got was a colossal shock to her system. Furious callers raged down the line at her and several staff appeared in person to remonstrate with her.

'A switchboard operator must remain calm,' Milly Sharpe reproved when Lizzie was as wrung out as a rag, jumping and flinching at the mere sight of an incoming call and ducking behind the screen if anybody walked past in case they were about to direct a volley of complaints at her.

She was weak with relief when she was switched to photocopying duties after lunch. Although the machine's sensors gave her a real fright by buzzing into sudden life the instant she approached, she felt better able to cope. In addition, something more than mere nerves was afflicting her: the longer she stood, the more light-headed she felt and her queasy tummy had put her off eating any lunch. She prayed that she was not developing summer flu.

Having access to a computer that was linked to the colour photocopier, while she waited for the copier to finish printing she succumbed to the temptation of doing an online search for information on Sebasten. But the very site she found brought up a to-die-for portrait photo of Sebasten and she never got any further. Her heartrate quickening at first glimpse of that lean, strong face, she drank in his image with intense appreciation. The stress of her difficult day seemed to evaporate as she hit the print button to get a copy of that photo to take home.

When *more* than one photo began to pile up in the copier, she did not initially panic. In fact she just thought she would have a photo for every handbag, would indeed not need to go an hour without a frequent fix of studying Sebasten. However, as the pile began to mount beyond the number of bags that even *she* possessed she tried to cancel the print run. But nothing she did would persuade the wretched machine to cease the operation. As luck would have it, Milly Sharpe arrived at that point.

Scooping up the first picture of Sebasten, she held it up

like an exhibit at a murder trial, icy condemnation in her challenging gaze. 'Where did you get this from?'

'I only meant to print one—'

'You mean…there's *more* than one?' the redhead demanded and swooped on the fat pile in disbelief, checking the print run with brows that vanished below her fringe. 'You have printed four *hundred* copies of this photo?'

Lizzie reddened to her hairline, feeling like a kid caught languishing over a secret pin-up. 'I'm really very sorry—'

'Have you any idea how much this special photographic paper costs per *single* sheet?'

Lizzie was shattered to be informed that she had wasted a couple of hundred pounds of very expensive stationery.

'*And* on company time!' The other woman's voice shook with outrage. 'I would also add that I consider it the height of impertinence to print photos of Mr Contaxis. I think it would be best if you spent the rest of the afternoon tidying up the stationery store room across the corridor.'

Just when Lizzie was wondering why it should be 'impertinent' to print images of Sebasten, a wave of such overpowering nausea assailed her that she was forced to bolt for the cloakroom. After a nasty bout of sickness she felt so dizzy that she had to hang on to the vanity counter before she felt steady enough on her feet to freshen up. While she was doing that, a slight, youthful blonde came in.

'I'm Rosemary. I'm to check up on you and show you to the sick room,' she explained with a friendlier smile than Lizzie had so far received from any of the female staff.

'I'm fine now,' Lizzie asserted in haste, thinking that if she ended up in the sick room on top of such a disastrous work performance, her first day would definitely be her *last* day of employment in the building.

'You're still very pale. Don't let Milly Sharpe get to you,' the chatty blonde advised. 'If you ask me, she's just got a chip on her shoulder about how you got your job.'

Lizzie frowned. '*How*...I got my job?'

Rosemary shrugged a carefully noncommittal shoulder. 'There's this mad rumour flying round that you didn't come in by the usual selection process but got strings pulled for you by someone influential on the executive floor—'

Lizzie coloured in dismay. 'That's not true—'

'The average temp doesn't wear delectable designer suits either and we're all killing ourselves over what you did with the photocopier,' Rosemary confided with an appreciative giggle as they left the cloakroom. 'Four hundred copies of our hunky pin-up boss, Sebasten. I bet Milly takes them home and papers her bedroom walls with them! Glad you're feeling better.'

'*Boss?*' Lizzie queried that astonishing label several seconds too late, for the blonde had already disappeared into one of the offices and Lizzie was left alone, fizzing with alarm and confusion.

She hastened into the stationery store room and yanked her mobile phone from her bag to punch out Sebasten's personal number. When he answered, she broke straight into harried speech. '*Am* I working for you?'

'Yes...did you finally get to read a letterhead?' Sebasten murmured with silken mockery. 'CI stands for Contaxis International.'

'Did you *fix* this job for me?' Lizzie demanded with a sinking heart, devastated by that first confirmation.

'You wouldn't have got it on your own merits,' Sebasten traded, crushing her with that candid assessment. 'Personnel don't take risks when they hire junior employees even on a temporary basis.'

'Thanks...' Lizzie framed shakily and then with angry stress continued. '*Thanks* for treating me like an idiot and not telling me that this was your company! *Thanks* for embarrassing me to death by doing it in such a way that the staff here know that I got preferential treatment!'

'Anything else you want to thank me for?' Sebasten

enquired in an encouraging tone that was not calculated to soothe.

'I needed a job but you should have told me what you were doing!' Lizzie condemned furiously. 'I don't need your pity—'

'Trust me,' Sebasten drawled, velvety soft and smooth. 'The one emotion I do not experience in your radius is...pity. I'll pick you up at eight for the dinner party...OK?'

Lizzie thrust trembling fingers through the hair flopping over her damp brow. 'Has one thing I've said got through to you?'

'I'm not into phone aggro,' Sebasten murmured drily.

'I don't want to see you tonight—'

'I didn't hear that—'

'I...don't...want...to...see...you...tonight,' Lizzie repeated between clenched teeth, rage and pain gripping her in a vice that refused to yield. 'If you don't care about my feelings, I shouldn't *be* with you!'

'Your choice,' Sebasten breathed and cut the call.

After work, Lizzie returned to her bedsit in a daze. She stared at her fresh, daffodil-yellow walls, completed to perfection by the decorators he had hired. It was over, finished...just like that? Without ever seeing him again? Had she been unfair? Even downright rude and ungrateful? How long would it have taken her to find a job *without* his preferential treatment? She had no references, no office skills, no qualification beyond good A-level exam results gained when she was eighteen. In the following four years she had achieved nothing likely to impress a potential employer, although she had gone to great creative endeavours to try and conceal that fact on her application form.

When her father phoned her on her mobile phone out of the blue at seven that evening and asked her if she would like to meet him for dinner she was really pleased, for they had not spoken since she had left home. Over that meal, she made a real effort to seem cheerful. Felicity,

Maurice Denton then confided wearily, had demanded that he dismiss their housekeeper, Mrs Baines, and he didn't want to do it. The older woman had worked for the Dentons for over ten years and was very efficient, if somewhat dour in nature.

'I thought possibly you could have a quiet word with Felicity on the subject,' her parent completed hopefully.

'No, thanks. It's none of my business.' But, even so, Lizzie was curious as to what the housekeeper could have done to annoy Felicity and she asked.

'Nothing that I can see…' Maurice muttered with barely concealed irritation. 'To tell you the truth, sometimes I feel like I don't know my own wife any more!'

Sebasten went to the dinner party alone, smouldered in a corner for an hour with a group of men, listening to sexist jokes that set his teeth on edge, snubbed every woman who dared to so much as smile at him and left early. On the drive home, he decided he wanted to confront Lizzie.

When he pulled up in the street he was just in time to see Lizzie, sheathed in a little violet-blue dress that would have wowed a dead man, in the act of clambering out of a Porsche. Smiling as if she had won the lottery, she sped up onto the pavement to embrace the tall, well-built driver.

Maurice Denton returned his daughter's hug and sighed. 'Let's not leave it so long the next time. I'm really proud that you're managing on your own. I can't have got it as wrong as I thought with you.'

Lizzie was so busy keeping up her happy smile as her father drove off again that her jaw ached from the effort. In truth it had been an evening that provoked conflicting reactions inside her. Her father had let her see that his marriage was under strain. Once she would have been selfishly overjoyed by the news, but now she was worried, wondering if she had been a mean, judgemental little cat when it came to her stepmother. Felicity was pregnant and stressed out and surely *had* to be labouring under a burden of guilt and unhappiness?

'Busy night?' a familiar accented drawl murmured, breaking into Lizzie's uneasy thoughts with sizzling effect.

In bemusement, Lizzie spun round and just feet away saw Sebasten lounging back against the polished bonnet of a fire-engine-red Lamborghini Diablo. Instantly, she went into melt-down with relief: *he* had come to see *her*. Shimmering dark golden eyes lanced into hers.

'Sebasten...?' Lizzie tensed at the taut angularity of his hard features.

Like a jungle cat uncoiling prior to springing, Sebasten straightened in one fluid movement and strode forward. '*Theos mou*...you staged a deliberate fight with me today, didn't you?'

Her brow furrowed in confusion. 'Sorry?'

'You had *other* plans for tonight,' Sebasten grated, ready to ignite into blistering rage and only holding on to his temper while his intellect continued to remind him that he was in the street with a car-load of his own bodyguards sitting parked only yards away.

'I really don't know what you're talking about.' And Lizzie didn't, for she had already forgotten her father's brief presence while her brain strove to comprehend what Sebasten was so very angry about.

'You slut!' Sebasten bit out, lean hands coiled into powerful fists. 'I should've been waiting for this!'

Acknowledging that the volatile side of Sebasten that she had once considered so very appealing was in the ascendant, Lizzie sucked in a sustaining breath and murmured with determined calm. 'Could you lower your voice and say whatever it is you just said in—er—English?'

When Sebasten appreciated that he had spoken in Greek, incandescent rage lit up in his simmering gaze. He gave her the translation at sizzling speed.

So taken aback was Lizzie by that offensive charge that she just stared at him for a count of ten incredulous seconds.

'And you're coming home with me so that we can have

this out in *private*!' Sebasten launched at her between even white gritted teeth.

A shaken little laugh with a shrill edge fell from Lizzie's parted lips. Even as pain that he should attack her out of the blue with such an unreasonable accusation assailed her, she could not credit that he should imagine that she would now go *any* place with him.

Without warning, Sebasten closed a purposeful hand to her elbow.

Temper finally igniting, for caveman tactics had never had even the smallest appeal to her, Lizzie slapped his hand away and backed off a pointed step. 'Are you crazy? What's got into you? I have a stupid argument with you and you come out of nowhere at me and call me a name like that?'

'I saw you smarming over the jerk in the Porsche! How long has *he* been around?' Sebasten raked at her, all awareness of surroundings now obliterated by a fury stronger than any he had ever experienced.

At that point, clarification was shed on the inexplicable for Lizzie: he was talking about her father. Green eyes sparkling, she tilted her chin. 'Since before I was born. My father looks well for his age, doesn't he? But then he keeps himself very fit.'

'Since before you were *born*…your father?' Sebasten slung before the proverbial penny dropped, as it were, from a very great height on him.

'Goodnight, Sebasten,' Lizzie completed and she swanned into the terraced building behind him with all the panache and dignity of a queen.

Out on the pavement, Sebasten turned the air blue with bad language and then powered off in immediate pursuit.

When a knock that made the wood panels shake sounded on the door of her bedsit, Lizzie opened it on the security chain and peered out. 'Go away,' she said fiercely. 'How dare you insult me like that? And how dare you call my father a jerk?'

Before Sebasten had the opportunity to answer either furious demand, the door closed again in his face. Her father. What he had witnessed was the innocent family affection of a father and daughter. The mists of rage were dimming only to be replaced by a seething awareness that he had got it wrong. And she had *laughed*. Lean, whipcord muscles snapping to rigidity as he recalled that shrill little laugh, Sebasten went home and collected a speeding ticket on the way.

In the bath that Lizzie took to wind down, she ended up humming happily to herself. True, she had been furious with Sebasten, but Sebasten had been beside himself with rage only because he was *jealous*. No man had ever thrown a jealous scene over Lizzie before and she could not help but be impressed by the amount of emotion Sebasten had put into that challenge. For the first time in her life, she felt like an irresistible and dangerous woman. Just imagine Sebasten getting that worked up over the belief that she was two-timing him! Lizzie smiled and smiled. But he just had to learn what was acceptable and what wasn't. He wasn't very trusting either, was he? However, he did seem pretty keen. He would phone her, wouldn't he? Should she just have let him come in?

The following morning, Lizzie wakened feeling out of sorts again and groaned with all the exasperation of someone rarely ill. Perhaps she had picked up some bug that her system couldn't shake off. About that point, she registered that, although she had finished taking her contraceptive pills for that month, her period had still not arrived and she tensed. No, she couldn't possibly be pregnant! Why was she even thinking such a crazy thing? All the same, accidents did happen, she reasoned anxiously and she decided to buy a testing kit at lunchtime just to *prove* to herself that she had nothing to worry about.

When she arrived at Contaxis International, she was taken down to the basement file-storage rooms with an entire trolley-load of documents to be filed away. As Milly

Sharpe smiled after showing her the procedure with her own personal hands, Lizzie had the sneaking suspicion that the subterranean eerie depths of the building were where she was destined to stay for the remainder of her three-month contract.

Footsteps made a creepy hollow sound in the long, quiet corridors and Lizzie had a rich imagination. She peered out of the room she was in: there was a security guard patrolling. As she worked, she heard occasional distant noises and indistinct echoes. With the exception of the older man parked at a desk with a newspaper at the far end of the floor, there seemed to be nobody on permanent duty in the basement. It was boring and lonely and she hated it but she knew she had to stick it out. Not having made a good start the day before, she reckoned she was still lucky to be employed.

When she heard brisk footsteps ringing down the corridor just before lunchtime, she assumed it was the security guard again until she heard her own name called loud and clear and setting up a train of echoes. 'Lizzie!'

It was Sebasten's voice and he was in no need of a public-address system, for, having done an initially discreet but fruitless search of half a dozen rooms for her, he was out of patience. He had ensured that a magnificent bouquet of flowers had been delivered to her early that morning and he had expected her to phone him.

Lizzie ducked her head round the door. 'What are you *doing* down here?'

'This is my building—'

'Show-off,' she muttered, colour rising into her cheeks as she allowed herself to succumb to the temptation of looking at him.

'Isn't this a great place for a rendezvous?' Sebasten leant back against the door to shut it, sealing them into privacy.

'I don't think you should come looking for me when I'm at work,' Lizzie said with something less than conviction, for in truth she was pleased that he had made the effort.

From the crown of his proud dark head to the soles of his no doubt handmade shoes, he looked utterly fantastic, Lizzie acknowledged, the flare of her own senses in response to his vibrant, bronzed virility leaving her weak. His charcoal-grey business suit exuded designer style and tailoring. His shadow-striped grey and white shirt would have an exclusive monogram on the pocket: she ought to know, after all; she had two of them in her possession and had no intention of returning them.

As Sebasten began at her slender feet and worked his bold visual path up over her glorious legs to the purple silk skirt and aqua tie top she wore, sexy, smouldering intent emanated from every lithe, muscular inch of his big, powerful body.

'Miss me...?' he enquired lazily.

'After the way you behaved last night? You've got to be joking!' Lizzie dared.

'How was I to know the guy with the Porsche was your father?' Sebasten demanded, annoyed that she was digging up a matter that he believed should be closed and forgotten.

'You could have given me the benefit of the doubt and just come over and spoken to us.' With unusual tact, Lizzie swallowed the 'like anybody normal would have done' phrase she had almost fired in addition.

Sebasten dealt her a level look golden eyes now dark, hard and unapologetic. 'I don't give women the benefit of the doubt.'

Lizzie stiffened. 'Then you must've known some very unreliable women but that's still not an excuse for throwing a word like "slut" at me!'

'What I saw looked *bad*,' Sebasten growled, evading the issue.

'Did you have a really nasty experience with someone?' Lizzie was dismayed by his stubborn refusal to apologise but far more disturbed by that initial statement of distrust in her sex.

'Oh, just a mother and three stepmothers,' Sebasten imparted with acid derision, dark eyes burning back to gold in warning.

'*Three?*' Her lush mouth rounded into a soundless circle and slowly closed again, for she was so disconcerted she could think of nothing to say.

'One gold-digger, two sluts and one pill-popper,' Sebasten specified with raw scorn, for he loathed any reference to his family background. 'I suppose you now think you understand me.'

No, what she understood was how deep ran his distrust and his cynicism and she was shaken by what he had kept hidden behind the sophisticated façade. Well, you admired the complexity and now you've got it in spades, a dry little voice said inside her head. This is the guy you love: running in the opposite direction is not a realistic option. What was in her own heart and the reality that she already ached at the thought of the damage done to him would pull her back.

'No, I think you'll do just about anything, even spill the beans about the family from hell...*anything* rather than apologise,' Lizzie quipped, making her tense mouth curve into a rueful grin.

Thrown by that unexpected sally, Sebasten stared down into her dancing green eyes, the worst of his aggressive tension evaporating. 'The flowers were the apology—'

'What flowers?'

'You should've got them this morning—'

'I leave for work at the crack of dawn.' Lizzie tossed her head back. 'Was there a card with a written apology included?'

'Just a signature,' Sebasten admitted, sudden raw amusement sending a slashing smile across his lean dark face. 'You're very persistent, aren't you?'

The megawatt charm of that smile made Lizzie's knees

wobble. Her body was held fast by a delicious tension that made her skin prickle, her breasts swell and her nipples tighten with sudden urgent and embarrassing sensitivity. 'Don't try to change the subject,' she warned him shakily.

'Or persuade you into silence?' Sebasten questioned, closing his hands to her narrow waist and lifting her up to bring her down on the table at which she had been sitting sorting documents just minutes earlier.

'Sebasten...' she gasped, disconcerted by that sudden shift into lover mode but secretly thrilled by it too. 'Suppose someone comes in?'

'The door's locked—'

'That was sneaky—'

'Sensible...' Sebasten contradicted, bracing long fingers either side of her and leaning forward to claim a teasing kiss. But the instant his mouth touched the lush softness of hers, he remembered how he had felt the night before when he had seen her in another man's arms and a sudden primitive need that was overwhelming swept him in stormy reaction. Instead of teasing, he forced her willing lips apart with the hungry driving pressure of his own.

Her heart banging in both surprise and excitement at his passion, Lizzie only worked up the will-power to tear free when her lungs were near to bursting. 'We have serious stuff to talk about—'

'This is *very* serious, *pethi mou*,' Sebasten broke in with fierce intensity, brilliant eyes locked to her as he let his lean hands travel with possessive appreciation up over her slender thighs. 'It was two weeks since we'd made love...two weeks of indescribable frustration...I think that must be why I lost my head last night.'

With a mighty effort of will Lizzie planted her hands in a staying motion over his, even though every weak, sinful skin-cell she possessed was thrumming like a car engine being revved. 'We haven't even discussed you fixing up this job for me—'

'But I'm so bloody grateful I did...it keeps you within

reach,' Sebasten groaned, escaping her attempt at restraint with single-minded purpose and sinking his hands beneath her hips instead to tug her to the edge of the table and lock her into contact with him.

Brought into tantalising connection with the virile thrust of his potent masculine arousal, Lizzie uttered a sudden moan and plunged both hands into his luxuriant black hair and kissed him with all the wild hunger she had suppressed during his absence unleashed. Sebasten sounded a raw, appreciative groan low in his throat. Throwing back his broad shoulders to remove his jacket, he jerked loose his silk tie with a distinct air of purpose and cast both away.

Her mouth ran dry even as shock gripped her that he intended to take their lovemaking further.

'I'm so hot for you, I *ache*,' Sebasten spelt out hoarsely, golden eyes smouldering over her with burning intent, any hope of restraint wrested from him by the sheer charge of shaken anticipation he could see in her feverishly flushed face.

'Yes…me too,' Lizzie muttered, instinctively ashamed of the intensity of her own hunger for him but unable to deny it.

With deft fingers Sebasten undid the tie on her aqua top, spread it wide and then tipped her back over one strong arm to claim a plundering kiss of raw, sensual urgency while he unclipped the front fastening on her white bra. 'I'm not used to frustration…I've never felt this *desperate*,' he grated truthfully.

That same seething desperation had Lizzie in an iron hold. She was trembling, already breathing in short, shallow little spurts. The bra cups fell from her tender breasts and a lean brown hand captured an erect pink nipple to toy with first one throbbing peak and then the other. The pleasure was hot, heady and so immediate that all the breath was forced from her in a long, driven gasp. The maddening twist of craving low in her belly was a growing torment.

Sebasten sat her up, sank impatient hands beneath her and peeled off her panties. She was helpless in the grip of her own abandonment. An earthy sound of approbation was wrenched from him when he discovered the slick satin heat already awaiting him, and from that point control no longer existed for him either.

'Please…' Lizzie heard herself plead in helpless thrall to the pleasure and to him.

Sebasten straightened, hauled her back to him at the point where she had all the resistance of a rag doll and sank into her silken sheath in one forceful thrust. She clung to him on a wave of such powerful excitement, she thought she might pass out with the sheer overload of sensation. It was wild, wilder than she had ever dreamt it could be even with him. When she finally convulsed in almost agonised ecstasy, he silenced her cry of release with the hot demand of his mouth, stilled the writhing of her hips and ground deep into her one last time.

In the wake of the most explosive climax of his life, Sebasten was stunned. He took in his surroundings, his attention lodging in disbelief on the bland office walls, and he was even more stunned. Feeling as though he had just come out of a blackout, he raised Lizzie, smoothed her silky, tumbled hair back from her brow with a hand he couldn't keep steady and began to restore her clothing to order at speed.

The loud staccato burst of knocking on the door froze him into stillness.

Dragged from the dazed aftermath of their intimacy, Lizzie opened shattered eyes wide on the aghast awareness of how impossible it would be to hide a male of six feet four inches in a room full of wall-to-wall filing cabinets. 'Oh, no…there's someone wanting t-to get in here—'

'Ignore it.'

'We can't!' she whispered frantically.

'We *can*—'

'I'm calling Security if this door is not unlocked immediately!' a furious female voice threatened from the corridor.

CHAPTER SIX

SEBASTEN swore under his breath, swept up his jacket and dug his arms into it while Lizzie leapt off the table, smoothed down her mussed skirt and retrieved the one item of her clothing which Sebasten had removed with a face that burned hotter than any fire.

'This is Sebasten Contaxis...the lock's jammed and I'm stuck in here! Call Maintenance!'' Sebasten called back, all ice-cool authority.

Five seconds later, high-heeled shoes were to be heard scurrying down the corridor. As soon as the racket of the woman's retreat receded, Sebasten stepped back and aimed a powerful kick at the lock. The door sprang open all on its own but the lock now looked damaged enough to support his story. Lizzie was still paralysed to the spot, transfixed by his speed and inventiveness in reacting to what had threatened to be the most humiliating encounter of her entire life.

'After you...' Sebasten invited with the shimmering golden eyes of a male who enjoyed a healthy challenge and enjoyed even more turning in a gold-medal performance for the benefit of an impressed-to-death woman. 'Grab a few files and lose yourself at the other end of the floor. I'll pick you up at half-six. We're entertaining tonight at Pomeroy Place, my country house, so pack a bag.'

'Sounds great,' she mumbled, revelling in the coupley togetherness of that 'we' he had employed.

'I forgot about the blasted party,' Sebasten admitted with a frown over that same slip of the tongue as he swung away.

'Sebasten...?' In a sudden surge of emotion that Lizzie

99

could no more have restrained than she could have held back floodwater, she flung herself at him as he turned back with an enquiring ebony brow raised. Green eyes shining, she linked her arms round his neck and gave him a hug. 'That's for just b-being you,' she told him, her voice faltering as he tensed in surprise.

'Thanks.' Sebasten set her back from him, his keen dark gaze veiling as he read the soft, vulnerable look in her expectant face. 'I should get going,' he pointed out.

Lizzie gathered up some loose papers and found another room in which to work. From there she could hear the rise and fall of speculative voices as maintenance staff attended to the damage door further down the corridor but she was incapable of listening. She pressed clammy hands to her pale, stricken face, unable to combat the deep inner chill spreading through her. Even after the incredible passion they had shared, even while her wretched body still ached from the penetration of his, her affectionate hug and declaration had been received like a step too far. He might have attempted to conceal that reality but his lack of any true response had spoken for him.

But why? For a split-second, Sebasten had looked down into her eyes and what had he seen there? *Love?* She felt humiliated, foolish and scared all at once. Whatever he had seen, he had not wanted to see. It was as though she had crossed some invisible boundary line and, instead of moving to meet her, he had turned his back. But then what had she been thinking of when she threw herself at him like that? The wildness of their lovemaking had shattered her and perhaps she had wanted reassurance…emotional reassurance.

At that awful moment of truth, Lizzie regretted her first night in Sebasten's bed with an angry self-loathing of her own weakness that nothing could have quenched. She had been reckless and now she was paying the price for not resisting temptation until she knew him better. Even more did she suffer at the recollection of her own wanton response to him only thirty minutes earlier. What Sebasten wanted it seemed Sebasten got. He touched her and she demonstrated all the self-will of a clockwork toy. For the first time, she understood with painful clarity just how cruelly deceptive sexual intimacy could be. Was she at heart the slut he had called her? She winced, her throat aching, because she was just so much in love with him. But did Sebasten see her as anything more than a casual sexual affair?

In the mood Lizzie was in, the prospect of devoting her lunch hour to buying a pregnancy test had scant appeal. Where had the insane fear that she might have conceived come from in the first place? It wasn't as though she had felt sick or even dizzy since she had come into work. She was just being silly, working herself up into a panic because she was involved in her very first intimate relationship. All the same, oughtn't she to check just to be on the safe side?

She bought the test kit, buried it in her bag, tried to forget it was there and discovered she could not. Then that afternoon, when she sprang up in a sudden movement after leafing through a bottom file drawer, her head swam and she swayed. As soon as she got home she knew she would use the test because a creeping sense of apprehension was growing at a steady rate at the back of her mind.

On the top floor of the CI building, Sebasten stared out at the city skyline with a brooding distance etched in his grim gaze. He was in a state of angry conflict that was foreign to him. *What was he playing at with Lizzie Denton?* When had his own motivations become as indistinct to him as a fog? Since the morning he learned her true identity, he had not once stopped to think through what he was doing in getting involved with her. That reality shook him at an instant when he was still striving without success to come up with an adequate explanation for what he had already labelled the 'basement episode'. He felt out of control and he didn't like it.

How could he keep on somehow neglecting to recall how cruelly Lizzie had treated his half-brother, Connor? Or the number of sweet studied lies that had tripped off her ready tongue on that same subject? What was he suffering from? Selective-memory syndrome? Did that glorious body of hers mean more to him than his own honour? Or even basic decency? From start to finish, his intimacy with her had defied every tenet he lived by.

He could no more easily explain why he had bought her diamonds and her car back for her. Did Lizzie deserve a reward for demonstrating that buckets of winsome pseudo-innocent charm could conceal a shallow nature? After all, most women made a special effort to impress and hide their worst side around a male of his wealth. Furthermore, he was very fond of Ingrid Morgan but he was bitterly aware that on the day of Connor's funeral he had made the rare mistake of letting emotions cloud his judgement. It was past time he ended what should *never* have begun...

While Sebasten was coming to terms with what he saw as an inevitable event, Lizzie was seated on her bed in shock, just staring at the little wand that had turned a certain colour ten minutes earlier. She picked up the test kit instructions and read the section on false results for the third time. Maybe the kit had been old stock. She checked the sell-by date on the packaging but there was no comfort to be found there.

Although it seemed incredible to her, she *was* going to have a baby...Sebasten's baby. If he reacted to a hug as if it were a marriage proposal, how would he react to a baby? She paled and shivered and wrapped her arms round herself. That first night she had told him that she was protected, had fully, confidently believed that she was, but hadn't she also known that no form of contraception yet existed that was a hundred per-cent effective?

The concept of having a child in her life transfixed Lizzie. As yet none of her former friends had children and discussing babies had always been considered deeply uncool. Lizzie had always kept quiet about the fact that she adored babies, had had to restrain herself from commenting in public about how seriously attractive some of them were and how insidious was the appeal of the shops that sold tiny garments. She stood up and studied her stomach in the mirror, sucked what little of it there was in…was there just the very faintest hint of it not going in quite as far as it once had? Registering what she was doing, she frowned in dismay at her inability to think sensible thoughts.

She wasn't married, she wasn't solvent, she didn't even have a proper job, and on being told the father of her baby would most probably demonstrate *why* he had such a bad reputation. He might try to deny that he was the father or he might assume that she would agree to a termination that would free him from the responsibility for her child. In fact, it would be extremely naïve of her to expect anything but a shocked and angry reaction from Sebasten. This was a guy who had told her that he *never* gave women the benefit of the doubt. In her situation that was not good news.

Here she was, living in a crummy bedsit, having come down in the world the exact same day she met a very rich man, and lo and behold…a few weeks later she would be telling him that she had fallen pregnant by him. Even to her that scenario did not look good. The least suspicious of men might have doubts about conception having been accidental in such circumstances, so the odds were that Sebasten would immediately think that he had been deliberately entrapped. An anguished groan escaped Lizzie.

She might really love Sebasten but she was getting acquainted with his flaws and her pride baulked at the prospect of putting herself in such a demeaning position. There was no good reason why she should make an *immediate* announcement though, was there? Wouldn't it make more sense to wait until she had at least seen a doctor?

Furthermore, that would give her more time to work out how best to broach the subject with Sebasten...

As Sebasten drove over to collect Lizzie, he cursed the necessity of their having to spend the night under the same roof at Pomeroy.

He was about to break off their relationship, so where had his wits been when he had made an inconvenient arrangement like that? But then he had since worked out exactly where his wits had been over the past three weeks: *Lost in lust*. Indeed, recalling his own extraordinary behaviour that same morning, his strong jawline took on an aggressive cast. Unbelievably, he had staged a clandestine sexual encounter at Contaxis International in the middle of his working day. All decent restraint had vanished the same instant he laid eyes on Lizzie's lithe, leggy perfection: he had had that door shut and locked within seconds.

So, in common with most single males with a healthy sex drive, Sebasten reasoned, he had proved to be a pushover when it came to the lure of a forbidden thrill. But that angle was cold consolation to a Greek who prided himself on the strength of his own self-discipline. Yet in that file room he had behaved like a sex-starved teenager who took advantage of every opportunity, no matter how inappropriate it might be. That demeaning image rankled even more.

It just went to show that a guy should never, *ever* relax his guard round a woman, Sebasten conceded in grim conclusion. Lizzie was an absolute powder-keg of sexual dynamite. Why else could he not keep his hands off her? Why else had he dragged her home with him only hours after meeting her?

After all, he had never been into casual encounters. Had anyone ever told him that he would some day sink to the level of sobering up a drunk woman and then falling victim to her supposed charms afresh, he would have laughed out loud in derision. Only now he wasn't laughing. After all, he had only got through the previous couple of weeks of self-denial by virtually staying out of the country and seeing her only in public places, he acknowledged with seething self-contempt.

When he picked up Lizzie he would be really cool with her and she would register that the end was nigh for herself. Exactly *why*, he asked himself then, was he agonising about something that had cost him only the most fleeting pang with other women?

Relationships broke up every day. She had ditched Connor without an ounce of concern, he reminded himself. But then how did he judge her for that when he had done pretty much the same thing himself? The rejected lover was hurt and what could anybody do about that? He recalled Lizzie's shining, trusting green eyes clinging to him and something in his gut twisted. He didn't want to hurt her.

Lizzie was still getting ready when Sebasten arrived.

'Are you always this punctual?' she groaned, hot, self-conscious colour burning her cheekbones as she evaded his gaze, for all she could think about at that instant was the pregnancy test that had come up positive.

'Always,' Sebasten confirmed, shrugging back a cuff to check his Rolex for good measure, determined to be difficult.

He looked grim, Lizzie registered, her heart skipping a beat as she noted the tautness of his fabulous bone-structure.

'I'll wait in the car,' Sebasten said drily, striving not to notice the way her yellow silk wrap defined her slender, shapely figure. For a dangerous split-second he thought of her as a gaily-wrapped present he couldn't wait to unwrap and the damage was done: his body reminded him with ferocious and infuriating immediacy that their stolen encounter earlier had only blunted the edge of his frustration.

'Don't be daft…I'll only be a minute.' Lizzie watched the faintest hint of dark colour score his chiselled cheekbones and wondered in dismay what on earth was the matter with him.

Desperate for any form of distraction that might lessen his awareness of the ache in his groin, Sebasten studied the open suitcase festooned with an enormous heap of garments as yet unpacked. He frowned. She was very disorganised and he was quite the opposite, so why was there something vaguely endearing about the harried, covert way she was now trying to squash everything into the case without regard for any form of folding whatsoever? He hated untidiness, he hated unpunctuality. Tell her it's over *now*, his intelligence urged him just as Lizzie looked up at him.

'You've had a lousy day, haven't you?' she guessed in a warm and sympathetic tone that snaked out and wrapped round Sebasten like a silken man-trap. 'Why don't you just sit down and chill out and I'll make you a cup of coffee?'

Disconcerted, Sebasten parted his lips. 'I—'

'I bet the traffic was appalling too.' Lizzie treated him to the kind of appreciative appraisal that implied he had crossed at least an ocean and a swamp just to reach her door and disappeared behind the battered wooden screen that semi-concealed the tiny kitchen area in one corner.

'Lizzie…' Sebasten felt like the biggest bastard in creation but what hit him with even more striking effect was the sudden acknowledgment that he did not *want* to dump Lizzie. Shattered by that belated moment of truth with himself, he snatched in a deep, shuddering breath.

'Yes?' She reappeared, her wide, friendly smile flashing out at him as she handed him a cup of coffee. 'What's your favourite colour?'

'Turquoise,' Sebasten muttered, struggling to come to terms with what he had refused to admit to himself all afternoon. It was as if she had put a spell on him the first night: he and his hormones had been haywire ever since. Yet there was no way on earth that he could add to Ingrid's grief by keeping the woman she blamed for Connor's death in his own life. And did he not owe more respect to his late brother's memory? Lizzie's only hold on him was sex, he reminded himself angrily. She was also an appalling liar and he ought to tell her that before they parted company.

Lizzie rustled through the wardrobe, grateful for the opportunity to occupy her trembling hands. She just had a bad feeling about the mood Sebasten was in. She could only equate his presence with having a big black thundercloud hanging overhead. Clutching a turquoise dress, she went behind the screen to change.

Never had the audible rustle and silky slither of feminine garments had such a provocative effect on Sebasten's libido. Out of all patience with himself, infuriated by the threatening volcano of opposing thoughts, urges and emotions seething inside him, he paced the restricted confines of the room until she was ready and said little after they had driven off in the Lamborghini.

'Do you like—children?' Lizzie shot at him then right out of the blue.

Already on red alert, Sebasten's defensive antenna lit up like the Greek sky at dawn. The most curious dark satisfaction assailed him as his very worst expectations were fulfilled. After just weeks, it seemed, she was dreaming of wedding bells. But that satisfaction was short-lived as it occurred to him that, possibly, he had given her grounds to believe she had him hooked like a fish on a line.

Hadn't he made a huge prat of himself when he saw her hugging her father? And what about all those phone calls he had made to her when he was abroad? Why had he felt a need to phone her every damn day he was away from her? And sometimes *more* than once. Not to mention activities that were the total opposite of cool and sophistication in the CI basement. She might well believe that he was infatuated with her.

'Children are all right...at a distance,' Sebasten pronounced, cool as ice.

Lizzie lost every scrap of her natural colour and caution might have warned her to keep quiet but she was quite incapable of listening to such promptings. 'What sort of answer is that?'

'They *can* look quite charming in paintings,' Sebasten conceded, studying the traffic lights with brooding concentration. 'But they're noisy, demanding and an enormous responsibility. I'm much too selfish to want that kind of hassle in my life.'

'I hope your future wife feels the same way,' was all that Lizzie in her shattered state could think to mutter to cover herself in the hideous silence that stretched.

'I'm not planning to acquire one of those either,' Sebasten confessed in an aggressive tone. 'If even my father couldn't strike gold *once* in four marriages, what hope have I?'

'None whatsoever, I should think, with your outlook,' Lizzie answered in a tight, driven reply. 'Of course, some women would marry you simply because you're loaded—'

'Surprise…surprise,' Sebasten slotted in with satiric bite.

'But personally speaking…' Lizzie's low-pitched response quivered with the force of her disturbed emotions and she was determined to have her own say on the subject…'not all the money in the world would compensate me for being deprived of children. I also think there's something very suspect about a man who dislikes children—'

'*Suspect?* In what way?' Sebasten demanded with wrathful incredulity, exploded from his already unsettled state of mind with a vengeance.

'But then, as you said, you're very selfish, but to my way of thinking…a *truly* masculine man would have a more mature outlook and he would appreciate that a life partner and the children they would share would be as rewarding as they were restricting.'

Sebasten was so incensed, he almost launched a volley

of enraged Greek at her. Who was she calling immature? And when had he said that he *disliked* children? A truly masculine man? His lean brown hands flexed and tightened round the steering wheel as he sought to contain his ire at her daring to question what every Greek male considered the literal essence of being.

'Your mind is narrow indeed,' he gritted, shooting the Lamborghini down the motorway at above the speed limit.

'You're entitled to your opinion.' Lizzie was wondering in a daze of shock how she could have been so offensive but not really caring, for what he had told her had appalled her. Dreams she had not even known she cherished had been hauled out into the unkind light of day and crucified. 'But please watch your speed.'

Deprived of even that minor outlet for his rage, Sebasten slowed down, lean, bronzed features set like stone. 'The minute my father, Andros, suffered a setback in business and her jetset lifestyle looked to be under threat, my mother demanded a divorce. She traded custody of me for a bigger settlement,' he bit out rawly. 'Although she had access rights, she never utilised them. I was only six years old.'

In an altogether new kind of shock, Lizzie focused her entire attention on his taut, hard profile. 'You never saw her again?'

'No, and she died a few years later. A *truly* feminine, maternal woman,' Sebasten framed with vicious intent. 'My first stepmother slept with the teenager who cleaned our swimming pool. She liked very young men.'

'Oh…dear,' Lizzie mumbled, bereft of a ready word of comfort to offer.

'Andros divorced her. His next wife spent most of their marriage in a series of drug rehabilitation clinics but still contrived to die of an overdose. The fourth wife was much younger and livelier and she was addicted to sex but *not* with an ageing husband,' Sebasten delivered with sizzling contempt. 'The night that my father suffered the humiliation of overhearing her strenuous efforts to persuade *me* into bed, he had his first heart attack.'

After that daunting recitation of matrimonial disaster, Lizzie shook her head in sincere dismay. 'Your poor father. Obviously he didn't have any judgement at all when it came to women.'

Not having been faced with that less than tactful response before, Sebasten gritted his even white teeth harder until it crossed his mind that there was a most annoying amount of truth in that comment. Throughout those same years, Ingrid, who would have made an excellent wife, had hovered in the background, at first hopeful, then slowly losing heart when she was never once even considered as a suitable bridal candidate by the man who had been her lover on and off for years. Why not? She had been born poor, had had to work for a living and had made the very great strategic error of sharing his father's bed between wives.

But how the hell had he got on to such a very personal subject with Lizzie? What was it about her? When had he ever before dumped the embarrassing gritty details of his background on a woman? He was furious with himself.

Given plenty of food for thought, Lizzie blinked back tears at the mere idea of what Sebasten must have suffered after his greedy mother's rejection was followed by the ordeal of three horribly inadequate stepmothers. Was it any wonder that he should be so anti-marriage and children? Her heart just went out to him and she was ashamed of her own face-saving condemnation of his views earlier. After all, what did she know about what *his* life must have been like? Only now, having been given the bare bones, she was just dying to flesh them out.

However, Sebasten's monosyllabic responses soon squashed that aspiration flat and silence fell until the Lamborghini accelerated up a long, winding drive beneath a leafy tunnel of huge weeping lime trees. Pomeroy Place was a Georgian jewel of architectural elegance, set off to perfection by a beautiful setting.

Before the housekeeper could take Lizzie upstairs, Lizzie glanced back across the large, elegant hall and focused with anxious eyes on Sebasten's grim profile before following the older woman up the superb marble staircase. Shown into a gorgeous guest room, she freshened up, a frown indenting her brow. In the mood Sebasten was in, he felt like an intimidating stranger. But then, it was evident that she had roused bad memories, but did he have to shut her out to such an extent? Could he not appreciate that she had feelings too?

Downstairs, receiving the first of his guests, Sebasten was discovering that a bad day could only get much worse when the vivacious gossip columnist Patsy Hewitt arrived on the arm of one of his recently divorced friends. Aware that Lizzie had been attacked by one of the tabloid newspapers for not attending Connor's funeral, the very last person he wanted seated at his dining-table was a journalist with a legendary talent for venom against her own sex. He did not want his relationship with Lizzie exposed in print just when he was about to end it. In fact, he was determined to protect Lizzie from that final embarrassment.

Quite how he could hope to achieve that end he had no clear idea, and then even the option seemed to vanish when Lizzie walked into the drawing room. He watched Patsy look at Lizzie and then turn back to the other couple she had been chatting to and he realised with relief that the journalist had no idea who Lizzie was.

'And this is Lizzie,' he murmured with a skimming glance in her general direction, drawing her to the attention of his other guests in a very impersonal manner.

'Do you work for Sebasten?' a woman in her thirties asked Lizzie some minutes later, evidently having no suspicion that Lizzie might be present in any other capacity.

'Yes.' The way Sebasten was behaving, Lizzie was

happy to make that confirmation but an angry, discomfited spark flared in her clear green eyes.

Another four people arrived and soon afterwards they crossed the hall to the dining room. Pride helped Lizzie to keep up her end of the general conversation but she did not look at Sebasten unless she was forced to do so. What she ate or even whether she *did* eat during that meal she was never later to recall. She started out angry but sank deeper into shock as the evening progressed. Had she really expected to act as his hostess? Certainly, she had not expected to be treated like someone merely invited to keep the numbers at the table even.

'So…which luscious lady are you romancing right now?' the older brunette, who had entertained them all with her sharp sense of humour, asked Sebasten in a coy tone over the coffee-cups.

Lizzie froze and watched Sebasten screen his dark eyes with his spiky black lashes before he murmured lazily. 'I'm still looking.'

With a trembling hand, Lizzie reached for her glass of water. Feeling sick, betrayed and outraged, she backed out of her chair without any perceptible awareness of what she was about to do, walked down the length of the table and slung the contents of her glass in Sebasten's face. 'When I find a real man, I'll let you know!' she spelt out.

Sebasten vaulted upright and thrust driven fingers through his dripping hair.

The silence that had fallen had a depth that was claustrophobic.

And then, as Lizzie went into retreat at the shimmering incredulity in Sebasten's stunned golden eyes, one of the guests laughed out loud and she spun to see who it was that could find humour in such a scene.

'Bravo, Lizzie!' Patsy Hewitt told her with an amused appreciation that bewildered Lizzie. 'I don't think I've *ever* enjoyed a more entertaining evening.'

'I'm glad someone had a good time,' Lizzie quipped

before she walked out of the room and sped upstairs with tears of furious, shaken reaction blinding her.

Had that guy talking been the guy she thought she loved? The male whose baby she carried? Denying her very existence? He was *ashamed* of her. What else was she to believe but that he was ashamed to own up to being involved with Connor Morgan's ex-girlfriend? He needn't think she had not eventually read the significance of his having neglected to speak her surname even once or his determination not to distinguish her with one atom of personal attention. So why the heck had he invited her? And how did she ditch him when she was expecting his baby?

But such concerns for a future that seemed distant were beyond Lizzie at a moment when all that was on her mind was leaving Sebasten's house just as fast as she could manage it. So it was unfortunate that while she had been downstairs dining her case had been unpacked.

She was in shock after the evening she had endured and the shattering discovery that Sebasten could turn into a male she really didn't want to know. Why? *Why* had he suddenly changed towards her?

In a flash, she recalled his cool parting from her that morning at Contaxis International and stilled, comprehension finding a path through her bewilderment. Nothing had been right since then. He had been in a distant mood when he came to pick her up and then in the car she had asked that stupid question about whether or not he liked children and the atmosphere had gone from strained to freezing point. He wanted *out*. Why had she not seen that sooner?

With nerveless hands, she dragged out her case and plonked it down on the bed. She remembered the way he had made love to her earlier in the day and she shivered, almost torn in two by the agony that threatened to take hold of her.

When Sebasten strode in, she was gathering up the items she had left out on the dressing-table earlier and in the act of slinging them willy-nilly into her case.

'What do you want?' Lizzie asked, refusing to look higher than his snazzy dark blue silk tie.

'Perhaps I don't like having water thrown in my face in front of an audience,' Sebasten heard himself bite out, although that had not been the tack he had planned to take. 'And the audience didn't much enjoy the fall-out either…it's barely midnight and they've all gone home.'

'If I had had anything bigger and heavier within reach, the damage would have been a lot worse!' Lizzie's soft mouth was sealed so tight it showed white round the edges.

'Do you even realise who the woman who last spoke to you *was*?'

'I don't know and I don't care. There is just no excuse for the way you treated me tonight!' Lizzie was fighting to retain a grip on her disturbed emotions and walk out on him with dignity. Deep down inside she knew that if she allowed herself to think about what she was doing or what was happening between then she might come apart at the seams in front of him.

'Patsy Hewitt is the *Sunday Globe*'s gossip columnist. No prizes for guessing which couple will star in her next lead story!'

The journalist's name had a vague familiarity for Lizzie but so intense was her emotional conflict that she could not grasp why he should waste his breath on something that struck her as an irrelevant detail.

'I didn't flaunt our relationship tonight because I wanted to protect you from that kind of unpleasant media exposure,' Sebasten completed angrily.

That *he* should dare to be angry with *her* after the way he had behaved added salt to the wounds he had already inflicted. In the back of her mind, she discovered, had lurked a very different expectation: that he might grovel for embarrassing her in such a way, for denying her like a Judas before witnesses. And nothing short of grovelling apologies would have eased the colossal pain of angry, bewildered loss growing inside her.

'Why the heck should a guy with *your* reputation care about media exposure?' Lizzie demanded and looked at him for the first time since he had entered the room.

And it hurt, it hurt so much to study those lean, devastatingly attractive features, note the fierce tension etched in his fabulous bone-structure and recognise the hard condemnation in his scorching golden eyes.

'And why the heck would I care anyway?' she added in sudden haste, determined to get in first with what she knew was coming her way. 'We're finished and I want to go home. You can call a taxi for me!'

'You can stay the night here. It would be crazy for you to leave this late at night.' Instead of being relieved that the deed he had been in no hurry to do had been done for him, a jagged shot of instant igniting fury leapt through Sebasten.

'The very idea of staying under the same roof as you is offensive to me. You're an absolute toad and I hope Patsy whatever-her-name-is shows you up in print for what you are!' Lizzie slung back not quite levelly, for a tiny secret part of her, a part that she despised, had hoped that he might argue with her announcement, might even this late in the day magically contrive to excuse his own behaviour and redress the damage he had done.

'Perhaps had you considered telling me the truth about Connor *this* might not be happening,' Sebasten heard himself declare, his jawline clenching hard. 'Instead you lied your head off to me!'

'I beg your pardon...?' Settling perplexed green eyes on him, Lizzie stared back at him, her heart beginning to beat so fast at that startling reference to Connor that it felt as if it was thumping inside her very throat. Why was he dragging Connor in?

'Connor's mother, Ingrid, is a close family friend.'

Her gaze widened in astonishment at that unexpected revelation, pallor driving away the feverish flush in her cheeks, an eerie chill tingling down her spine. 'You didn't tell me that before…you *said* you hardly knew him—'

'I knew Connor better as a child than as an adult.' On surer ground now, Sebasten let true anger rise and never had he needed anger more than when he saw the shattered look of incomprehension stamped to Lizzie's oval face. She was so pale that all seven freckles on her nose stood out in sharp relief. 'You also said you didn't know him well and then told repeated lies about your relationship with him.'

'I *didn't* lie,' Lizzie countered in angry bewilderment, her tall, slender body rigid as she attempted to challenge the accusation that she was a liar while at the same time come to terms with the shocking reality that Sebasten had close ties that he cherished with the Morgan family but that he had not been prepared to reveal that fact to her. 'I actually told you a truth that nobody other than myself, Connor and the woman involved knew!'

'*Theos mou*…the *truth*?' Sebasten slammed back with raw derision, infuriated that he had noticed her freckles in the middle of such a confrontation and outraged by the unfamiliar stress of having to fight to maintain his concentration. 'Your most ingenious story of Connor's secret affair with a married woman that would be impossible to disprove when you declined to name the lady involved. That nonsense was a base and inexcusable betrayal of Connor's memory!'

'You *didn't* believe me,' Lizzie registered in a belated surge of realisation and she shook her bright head in a numbed movement. 'And yet you never said so, never even mentioned that Ingrid Morgan was a friend of yours. Why did you conceal those facts? If you believed I was lying, why didn't you just confront me?'

'Maybe I thought it was time that someone taught you a lesson.' No sooner had Sebasten made that admission than he regretted it. 'That was *before* I understood that what I was doing to you was as reprehensible as what you did to Connor.'

Lizzie only heard that first statement and her blood ran cold in her veins. *Maybe I thought it was time that someone taught you a lesson.* That confession rocked her already shaken world and threatened to blow it away altogether. He had gone after her, singled her out, and it had *all* been part of some desire to punish her for what she had supposedly done to Connor? She was shattered by that final revelation.

'What sort of a man are you?' Lizzie demanded in palpable disbelief.

Anger nowhere within reach, Sebasten lost colour beneath his bronzed skin and fought an insane urge to pull her into his arms and hold her tight. 'The night I met you, the first night, I didn't *know* who you were. I didn't find out until the following morning when I saw your driving licence.'

Lizzie dismissed that plea without hesitation. 'I don't believe in coincidences like that…you went on the hunt for me.'

'Had I known who you were I would never have gone to bed with you,' Sebasten swore half under his breath.

A wave of dizziness assailed Lizzie. She could not bear to think of what he had just said. Blocking him from her mind and her view, she sank down on the foot of the bed and reached for her mobile phone. Desperate to leave his house, she punched out the number of a national cab firm to request a taxi.

'Hell…*I'll* take you back to London!' Sebasten broke in.

Having made the call, Lizzie ignored him and breathed in slow and deep to ward off the swimming sensation in her head. The guy she had fallen in love with had embarked on their relationship with the sole and deliberate intent of hurting and humiliating her. She could not believe that he could have been so cruel, and why? Over the head of Connor, who had already cost her so much!

Sick to the heart, she stood up like an automaton and headed for the dressing room, where she assumed her clothes had been stowed away. She dragged garments from hangers and drawers, dimly amazed at the amount of stuff she had contrived to pack for a single night. But then she had been in love, hadn't she been? Unable to make up her mind what she might need, what would look best, what *he* might admire most on her. A laugh that was no laugh at all bubbled and died again inside her. Her throat was raw and aching but, in the midst of what she believed to be the worst torture she would ever have to get through, her eyes were dry.

Sebasten hovered, lean, powerful hands clenching and unclenching. 'I should never have slept with you,' he admitted with suppressed savagery. 'If I could go back and change that I *would*—'

'Try staying out of basements too.' Her tone one of ringing disgust, Lizzie quivered with a combustible mix of self-loathing and shame that he could have been so ruthless and wicked as to take advantage of her weakness. 'There could never have been an excuse for what you've done. That you should have set out to cause me harm is unforgivable.'

'Yes,' Sebasten conceded in Greek, snatching in a deep-driven breath and switching back to English to state. 'I *do* accept that two wrongs do not make a right, but in the heat of the moment when I was confronted with the depth of Ingrid's despair my mind was not so clear. I was appalled that first morning when I discovered your true identity and what took place today was indefensible. But from the outset I was very much attracted to you.'

Heaping clothes into the case, Lizzie made herself look at him, hatred in her heart, hatred built on a hurt that went so deep it felt like a physical pain. 'Is that supposed to make me feel better? I met you when my whole life had crashed around me. I was very unhappy and you must have seen that…yet you waded in and made it worse,' she condemned. 'How could you be such a bastard?'

'I lost the plot…isn't that obvious?' Sebasten threw back at her with a savage edge to his accented drawl as he swept up the couple of garments she had dropped on her passage from the dressing room but held on to them because he did not want to hasten her departure. 'I got in deeper than I ever dreamt and I'm paying a price for that now too.'

Lizzie thought in a daze of the child she carried and a spasm of bitter regret tightened her facial muscles. She was no longer listening to him. 'Connor cheated on me and he didn't spare my feelings a single thought. I lost my friends and my father's respect. I paid way over the odds for being the fall guy in that affair. But this is something else again…I *loved* you…' Her voice faltered to a halt and she blinked, shocked that she had admitted that and then, beyond caring, she snapped her case closed with trembling hands and swung it down off the bed.

'I don't want you to leave in this frame of mind…' Sebasten declared as much to her as to himself.

'I hate you. I will never forgive you…so stop saying really *stupid* things!' Lizzie slung at him with a wildness that mushroomed up from within her without any warning and made her feel almost violent. 'What did you expect from me? That I was going to shake hands and thank you for wrecking my life again!'

Sebasten had no answer, but then he had never thought that far ahead and just then cool, rational thought evaded him. 'If you want to go back to London tonight, let me drive you,' he urged, taking refuge in male practicality.

'You're wired to the moon,' Lizzie accused shakily, hauling her case past him.

His hand came down over hers and forced her fingers into retreat from the handle. She just let him have the case. She walked to the door, threw it wide and started down the stairs while she willed the taxi to come faster than the speed of light.

Sebasten reached the hall only seconds in her wake. As a manservant hurried from the rear of the hall to relieve him of the case, only to be sent into retreat by the ferocious look of warning he received from his employer, Lizzie wrenched open the front door on her own.'

'Give me my case!' she demanded, fired up like an Amazon warrior.

With pronounced reluctance, Sebasten set the case down. 'Lizzie…Connor was my half-brother…'

Lizzie spun back to him in astonishment and an image of Connor surged up in her mind's eye: the very dark brown eyes that had been so unexpected with her ex-boyfriend's blond hair, the classic bone-structure, his height and build. She did not question Sebasten's ultimate revelation. Indeed, for her it was as though the whole appalling picture was finally complete.

'*Two* of you…' she muttered sickly as she turned away again to focus with relief on the car headlights approaching the front of the house. 'And *both* of you arrogant, selfish, lying rats who use and abuse women! Now, why doesn't that surprise me?'

Sebasten froze at that response. The cab driver got out to take her case. Within the space of a minute, Lizzie was gone. Sebasten looked down at the flimsy white bra and red silk shirt he was still grasping in one hand and he knew that he was about to get so drunk that he didn't know what day it was.

CHAPTER SEVEN

LIZZIE didn't cry that night: she was reeling with so much shock and reaction she was exhausted and she lay down on her bed still clothed and fell asleep.

After only a few hours, she wakened to a bleak sense of emptiness and terrible pain. She had fallen in love with a sadist. Sebasten had got under her skin when she was weak and vulnerable and hurt her beyond relief. Yet he was also the father of her baby. Her mind shied away from that daunting fact and her thoughts refused to stay in one place.

If Sebasten was Connor's half-brother that meant that the still attractive Ingrid must have had an affair with Sebasten's father. A very secret affair it must have been, for Connor himself when she asked had told Lizzie a different story about the circumstances of his birth.

'Ingrid met up with an old flame and the relationship had fizzled out again before she even knew I was on the way,' he had confided casually. 'He was an army officer. She did plan to tell him when he came back from his posting abroad but he was killed in a military helicopter crash shortly before I was born.'

Had that tale been a lie? Her brow indented as she dragged herself out of bed to look into her empty fridge. What was the point of thinking about Connor and the blood tie that Sebasten had claimed? She needed to keep busy, she told herself dully. She also had to eat to stay healthy, which meant that she had to shop even when the very thought of food made her feel queasy. In addition, she reminded herself, she had to make an appointment with the doctor.

Without ever acknowledging that she was still so deep in shock from the events of the previous twenty-four hours that she could barely function, Lizzie drove herself through that day. She got a cancellation appointment at the doctor's surgery. She learned that she was indeed pregnant and when she asked how that might have happened when she had been taking contraceptive pills was asked if she missed taking any or had been sick. Instantly she recalled that first night with Sebasten when she had been ill, stilling a shiver at the wounding memories threatening her self-discipline, she fell silent. Concentration was impossible. Behind every thought lurked the spectre of her own grief.

From the medical centre she trekked to the supermarket, where she wandered in an aimless fashion, selecting odd items that had more appeal than others, but she returned to her bedsit and discovered that she had chosen nothing that would make a proper meal. She grilled some toast, forced herself to nibble two corners of it before having to flee for the bathroom and be ill.

Sebasten rose on Sunday with a hangover unlike any he had ever suffered. He had virtually no memory of Saturday. Any thought of Lizzie was the equivalent of receiving a punch to the solar plexus but he couldn't get her haunting image out of his mind. Was it guilt? What else could it be? When had any Contaxis ever sunk low enough to contemplate taking revenge on a woman? What the hell had got into him that he had even considered such a course of action? And now, when he was genuinely worried about Lizzie's state of mind, how could he check up on her?

Over breakfast, he flipped open the gossip page of the *Sunday Globe* and any desire to eat receded as he read the startling headline: 'CONTAXIS 0, DENTON 10.'

For all of his adult life, Sebasten had been adored and fêted and flattered by the gossip-column fraternity but Patsy Hewitt's gleeful account of events at his dinner party was very much of the poison-pen variety and directed at *him*. She made him sound like a total arrogant bastard and recommended that Lizzie keep looking until she found a man worthy of her, a piece of advice which sent Sebasten straight into an irrational rage.

Of course Lizzie wasn't about to race off on the hunt for another man! She was in love with him, wasn't she? But since their affair was over, ought he not to be keen for her to find a replacement for him? Just thinking about Lizzie in another man's bed drove Sebasten, who ate a healthy breakfast every morning without fail, from the breakfast table before he had had anything more than a single cup of black coffee.

He went out for a ride, returned filthy and soaked after a sudden downpour and got into the shower. After that, he tried to work but he could not concentrate. Why shouldn't he be concerned about Lizzie? He asked himself defensively then. Wasn't he human? And why shouldn't he give her the Mercedes and the diamonds back? After all, what was he to do with them? She was having a hard time and possibly getting back the possessions which she had been forced to sell would cheer her up a little.

As for her father, Maurice Denton, *well*, Sebasten was starting to cherish a very low opinion of a man he had never met. Family were supposed to stick together through thick and thin and forgive mistakes. Instead the wretched man had deprived his daughter of all means of support when it was entirely *his* fault that she was quite unequal to the task of supporting herself in the style to which her shortsighted parent had encouraged her to become accustomed.

Inflamed on Lizzie's behalf by that reflection, Sebasten snatched up his car keys and arranged for the Mercedes to be driven back to London to be delivered. He could not wait long enough for his own car to be driven round to the front of the house and he startled his staff by striding through the rear entrance to the garages and extracting his Lamborghini for himself.

After attending church, guiltily aware that it was her first

visit since she had left home, Lizzie wondered why her
father and Felicity were absent from their usual pew and
realised that they must be spending the weekend at the
cottage. Buying a newspaper before she went back to the
bedsit, Lizzie read what Patsy Hewitt had written about
that evening at Pomeroy Place and assumed that the journalist had decided to take a feminist stance for a change.
She frowned when she perused the final cliff-hanging comment that advised readers to watch that space for a bigger
story soon to break and then assumed that it could be nothing to do with either her or Sebasten.

Studying Sebasten's lean, dark, devastating face in the
photo beside the article, her eyes stung like mad. Angry
with herself, she crushed the newspaper up in a convulsive
gesture and rammed it in the bin. Then she opened the
post that she had ignored the day before and paled at the
sight of a payment request from an exclusive boutique
where she had a monthly account. She had barely had
enough cash left in her bank account to cover travel ex-
penses and eat until the end of the month, when she would
receive her first pay cheque. She would have to ask for a
little more time to clear the bill. Furthermore, she would
have to exert bone and sinew to try and find part-time
evening or weekend employment so that she could keep
up her financial commitments.

The first Lizzie knew of the mysterious reappearance of
the Mercedes she had sold was the arrival of a chauffeur
at her door. 'Miss Denton…your car keys,' he said, hand-
ing them to her.

'Sorry?' Lizzie stared at him in bewilderment. 'I don't
own a car.'

'Compliments of Mr Contaxis. The Merc is parked outside.'

Before Lizzie even got her breath back, the man had
clattered back down the stairs again.

Compliments of Mr Contaxis? What on earth was going
on? In a daze, Lizzie left her room and went outside. There

sat the same black glossy Mercedes four-wheel-drive which her father had bought her for her twenty-second birthday. She couldn't credit the evidence of her own eyes and she walked round it in slow motion, her mind in a feverish whirl of incomprehension.

Where had Sebasten got her car from and why would he give it back to her? Why would a guy who had dumped her only thirty-six hours earlier suddenly present her with a car worth thousands of pounds? Oh, yes, she knew that—technically speaking—she had dumped him first but in her heart she accepted that she had only got the courage to do that because she had known that he intended to do it to her if she did not.

Having reclaimed the diamonds from the safe in his town house, Sebasten arrived on Lizzie's doorstep, feeling much better than he had felt earlier in the day, indeed, feeling very much that he was doing the right thing.

Lizzie opened the door. The sheer vibrant, gorgeous appeal of Sebasten in sleek designer garments that exuded class and expense exploded on her with predictable effect. Just seeing him hurt. Seeing him dare to *almost* smile was also the cruel equivalent of a knife plunging beneath her tender skin. Even an almost smile was an insult, a symptom of his ruthless, cruel, nasty character and his essential detachment from the rest of humanity.

Lizzie dealt him a seething glance. 'You get that car taken away right now!' she told him. 'I don't know what you think you're playing at but I don't want it.'

Engaged in looking Lizzie over in a head-to-toe careful appraisal that left not an inch of her tall, shapely figure unchecked and thinking that he might like the way turquoise set off her beautiful hair but that she did something remarkable for the colour red as well, Sebasten froze like a fox cornered in a chicken coop and attempted to regroup.

'I don't want your car either...it's no use to me,' he pointed out in fast recovery, closing the door and, without even thinking about what he was doing, leaning his big, powerful length back against that door so that she couldn't open it again.

'Exactly what are you doing with a car that I sold?' Lizzie demanded shakily, temper flashing through her in direct proportion to her disturbed emotions.

'I bought it back for you weeks ago…as well as these.' Sebasten set down the little pile of jewellery boxes on the table. 'I had you watched the first week by one of my bodyguards and I knew everything that you did.'

'You had me watched?' Lizzie echoed in even deeper shock and recoil as she flipped open a couple of lids to confirm the contents and the sparkle of diamonds greeted her. 'You bought my jewellery as well? *Why?*'

Sebasten had been hoping to evade that question. 'At the time I planned to win your trust and impress you with my generosity.'

'You utter bastard,' Lizzie framed with an agony of reproach in her clear green gaze. 'So that's why you offered me the use of an apartment! You thought you could tempt me with your rotten money. Well, you were way off beam then and you're even more out of line *now*—'

'I just want you to take back what's yours,' Sebasten slotted in with fierce determination.

'Why? So that you can feel better? So that you can *buy* your way out of having a conscience about what you did to me?' Lizzie condemned in a shaking undertone. 'Don't you even have the sensitivity to see that you're insulting me?'

'How…am I insulting you?' Sebasten queried between gritted teeth, for he was in no way receiving the response he had expected and he wondered why women always had to make simple matters complicated. He was trying to make her life easier. What was wrong with that?

'By making the assumption that I'm the kind of woman who would accept expensive gifts from a guy like you! How dare you do that? Do you think I was your mistress or something that you have to pay me off?' Lizzie was so worked up with hurt and anger that her voice rose to a shrill crescendo.

'No, but I never bought you a single thing during the whole time we were together,' Sebasten pointed out, one half of his brain urging him to take her in his arms and soothe her, the other half fully engaged in stamping out that dangerous temptation to touch her again.

'I suppose that's how you get so many women…you pay them with gifts for putting up with you!' Lizzie slung fiercely, fighting back the tears prickling at the backs of her eyes.

Determined not to react to that base accusation, Sebasten was staring down at the bill from the boutique that lay on the table and then studying the little column of figures added up on the sheet of paper beside it. Was she *that* broke?

'I could give you a loan. You would repay it when you could,' he heard himself say.

Lizzie wrenched open the door and said unsteadily. 'Go away…'

'It doesn't have to be like this.' Sebasten hovered, full of angry conflict and growing frustration. 'I came here with good motivations and no intention of upsetting you.'

Lizzie scooped up the jewel boxes and planted them in his hands along with the car keys. 'And don't you dare leave that car outside. I can't feed a parking meter for it on my income.'

'Lizzie—?'

'You *stay* away from me!'

'All I wanted to know was that you were OK!' Sebasten growled.

'Of course I'm OK. A visit from you is as good as a cure!' Lizzie hurled, her quivering voice breaking on that last assurance.

Sebasten departed. He should have thought about her not being able to afford to run a car, he reflected, choosing to focus on that rather than anything else she had said.

However, the disturbing image of her distraught face and the shadows that lay like bruises beneath her eyes travelled with him. She didn't look well. Was he responsible for that? For the first time since childhood Sebasten felt helpless, and it was terrifying. He could not believe how stubborn and proud she was. He saw Lizzie in terms of warmth and sunlight, softness and affection, and then he tried to equate that belated acknowledgement with the character that Ingrid had endowed her with.

Lizzie threw herself face down on the bed and sobbed into the pillow until she was empty of tears. What must her distress be doing to her baby? Guilt cut deep into her. She rested a hand against her tummy and offered the tiny being inside her a silent apology for her lack of control and told herself that she would do better in the future.

As for Sebasten, did she seem so pitiful that he even had to take her pride away from her by offering her a loan as well as the car and the diamonds? Why had she ever told him that she loved him? And why was he acting the way he was when all that she had ever known about him suggested that a declaration of love ought to drive him fast in the opposite direction? How dared he come and see her and make her feel all over again what she had lost when he wasn't worth having in the first place?

When was she planning to tell him about the baby? She drifted off to weary sleep on the admission that she was not yet strong enough to face another confrontational scene.

CHAPTER EIGHT

ON MONDAY morning, Sebasten thought his personal staff were all very quiet in his radius and he assumed that the *Sunday Globe* gossip column had done the rounds of the office.

He swore that he would not think about Lizzie. At eleven he found himself accessing her personnel file. When he discovered that she had been reprimanded for the printing of four hundred copies of a photo of himself, all hope of concentration was vanquished. He was annoyed that he liked the idea of those photos.

Sebasten did not believe in love. He was crazy about Lizzie's body…and her smile…and her hair. He had enjoyed the way she chattered too. She talked a lot, which in the past was a trait which had irritated him in other women, but Lizzie's chatter was unusually interesting. He had also liked the easy way she would reach out and touch him; nothing wrong with that either, was there? It didn't mean he was infatuated or anything of that nature, merely that he could still appreciate her good points.

On the other side of the equation, she was a rampant liar and she *must* have slept with his half-brother and he could not work out how he had managed to block that awareness out for so long. At the same time, he could no longer credit the dramatic contention that Lizzie had driven Connor to his death. Ingrid had needed someone to blame. But Connor had got behind the wheel of his car, drunk. That car crash had been the tragic result of his half-brother's recklessness and love of high speed.

At that point, without any prior thought on the subject that he was aware of, Sebasten decided to settle that outstanding bill he had seen in Lizzie's bedsit. She couldn't prevent him from doing that, could she?

That same day, Lizzie went into work and found herself the target of covert stares and embarrassing whispers. Only then did she recall the article that had been in the newspaper the previous day. In a saccharine-sweet enquiry, Milly Sharpe asked her where she would like to work and Lizzie reddened to her hairline.

'Any place,' Lizzie answered tautly and ended up at a desk in a corner where she was given nothing like enough to keep her occupied.

She saw then that continuing employment in Sebasten's company could well be less than comfortable for her. During her lunch break, she called into the employment agency across the road from the CI building and enjoyed a far more productive chat with one of the recruitment consultants there than she had received at the establishment which Sebasten had recommended a month earlier.

'You have a great deal of insider knowledge and experience in the PR field,' the consultant commented. 'I'm sure we can place you in a PR firm. It would be a junior position to begin with, and of course you're entitled to basic maternity leave, but if you prove yourself you could gain quite rapid advancement.'

On Tuesday, Sebasten took sudden note of how very long it had been since he had staged a meeting with the accounts team on the sixth floor and he instructed his secretary to make good that oversight. That Lizzie worked on that floor was not a fact he allowed to enter his mind once. On Wednesday, he was infuriated by the announcement that the accounts meeting could not be staged until Friday, as key personnel were away on a training course.

On Thursday, Ingrid phoned Sebasten and demanded to know if it was true that he had been seeing Liza Denton. Sebasten said it was but that it was a private matter not open to discussion, and if Ingrid's shock at that snub was perceptible Sebasten was equally disconcerted by the very real anger that leapt through him when the older woman then made an adverse comment about Lizzie. On Friday, Sebasten arrived at the office even earlier than was his norm, cleared his desk by nine, strode about the top floor unsettling his entire staff and checked his watch on average of once every ten minutes.

On the sixth floor, Lizzie's week had felt endless to her. She was craving Sebasten as though he were a life-saving drug and hating herself for being so weak. She knew she had to tell him that she was pregnant, but while she still felt so vulnerable she was reluctant to deal with that issue. Mid-week, during the extended lunch break she hastily arranged, she had an interview for a position with a PR firm but had no idea whether or not she was in with a chance. On Friday morning, Milly Sharpe greeted her arrival at work with a strange little smile and put her on the reception desk.

When Sebasten strode out of the lift, the first person he saw was Lizzie. Lizzie, clad in a yellow dress as bright as sunshine. He collided with her startled green eyes and walked right past the senior accounts executive waiting to greet him without even noticing the man.

'Lizzie…' Sebasten said.

Taken aback by his sudden appearance, Lizzie nodded in slow motion as though to confirm her identity while her gaze welded to him with electrified intensity. His sheer physical impact on her drove out all else. She drank him in, heart racing at the sudden buzz in the atmosphere and there was not a thought in her head that was worthy of an angry, bitter woman. His luxuriant black hair gleamed below the lights and her fingers tingled with longing. His brilliant golden eyes, semi-screened by his spiky lashes, set up a chain reaction deep down inside her, awakening the wicked hunger that melted her in secret places and made her tremble.

'So…' His mind a wasteland, his hormones reacting with a dangerous enthusiasm that made lingering an impossibility, Sebasten snatched in a deep, sharp breath. 'How are you?'

'OK…' Lizzie managed to frame after considerable effort to come up with that single word.

'I have a meeting…' Sebasten swung away, her image refreshed to vibrance in his memory.

As he strode down the corridor, Lizzie blinked and emerged from the spell he had cast. A slow, deep, painful tide of colour washed over her fair complexion. A burst of stifled giggles sounded from the direction of Milly Sharpe's office, which overlooked Reception, and her heart sank. Had she somehow shown herself up? Well, what else could she have done when she had just sat staring at Sebasten like a lovesick schoolgirl? Squirming in an agony of self-loathing and shame, Lizzie decided she would not be around when Sebasten emerged from his meeting again.

That afternoon the recruitment agency called and informed her that Robbins, the PR firm, were keen for her to start work with them the following week. Deep relief filled Lizzie to overflowing and she accepted the offer. Away from Contaxis International, she would be better able to put her life together again and possibly it would be easier to face telling Sebasten what he would eventually *have* to be told.

On Friday evening, for the sixth night in a row, Sebasten stayed home and brooded. He didn't want to go out and he didn't want company.

Lizzie called her father for a chat. He seemed very preoccupied and apologised several times for losing the thread of the conversation. She asked what he had decided to do about Mrs Baines, the housekeeper, whom Felicity had wanted dismissed.

Maurice Denton released a heavy sigh. 'I offered Mrs Baines a generous settlement in recognition of the number of years she'd worked for us. She accepted it but she was very bitter and walked out the same day. Felicity was delighted but I must confess that the whole business left a nasty taste in my mouth.'

'How is Felicity?'

'Very edgy…' the older man admitted with palpable concern. 'She bursts into tears if I even *mention* the baby and when I suggested that *I* ought to have a word with the gynaecologist she's been attending, she became hysterical!'

Lizzie raised her brows and winced in dismay. Was her stepmother heading for a nervous breakdown? All over again, she felt the guilty burden of the secret knowledge she was withholding from her father. Then she wondered how Maurice Denton, never the most liberal of men and very set in his traditional values, would react to a daughter giving birth to an illegitimate child and paled. Such an event might well sever her relationship with her father forever…

On Sunday morning, Sebasten again lifted the *Sunday Globe*, which he had always regarded as a rubbish newspaper aimed at intellectually-challenged readers. However, he only wanted to check out that Patsy Hewitt had not picked up any other information relating either to himself or Lizzie. The front page was adorned with the usual lurid headline offering the unsavoury details of some sleazy affair, he noted, and only at that point did he recognise that the article was adorned with a photo of Connor.

And Sebasten was gripped to that double-page spread inside the paper with a spellbound intensity that would have delighted Patsy Hewitt, who had found ample opportunity to employ her trademark venom after doing her homework on Lizzie's stepmother, Felicity Denton. Mrs Baines, the Denton housekeeper, had sold her insider story of Felicity's affair for a handsome price and Connor, even departed, still had sufficient news value to make the front page with his once tangled lovelife.

Lizzie was still in bed asleep when her mobile phone began ringing. Getting out of bed to answer it, she was bemused to realise that it was a former friend calling to express profuse apologies for misjudging her over Connor.

'What are you talking about?' she mumbled.

'Haven't you seen this morning's *Sunday Globe* yet?'

Learning that Mrs Baines had sold her story of Felicity's affair with Connor shook Lizzie rigid. No longer did she need to wonder why her stepmother had been so eager to get rid of the family housekeeper: Felicity had been justifiably afraid that Mrs Baines knew too much. Had Connor visited the Denton home as well? Lizzie wrinkled her nose with distaste. The housekeeper had probably known about that affair long before she herself did.

Over an hour later, Lizzie arrived at her family home to find it besieged by the Press. A half-dozen cameras flashed in her direction and she had to fight her way past to get indoors. Her father was sitting behind closed curtains in a state of severe shock.

CHAPTER NINE

'FELICITY walked out late last night. A friend in the media phoned to warn her about the story appearing in the *Sunday Globe*,' Maurice Denton shared in a shattered tone as Lizzie paced the room, too restive to stay still. 'Felicity isn't coming back. She made it clear that she wants a divorce.'

'But...but what about the baby?' Lizzie pressed, disconcerted by the speed and dexterity of her stepmother's departure from the marital home.

The older man regarded her with hollow eyes. In the space of days, he seemed to have aged. 'There *is* no baby...'

Lizzie's mouth fell wide. 'You mean, Felicity's lost it...oh, *no*!'

'There never *was* a baby. She wasn't pregnant. It was a crazy lie aimed at persuading you not to tell me about her affair with Connor.' Her parent shook his greying head with a dulled wonderment that he could not conceal. 'Felicity thought that if she *tried*, she could get pregnant easily and then pretend she'd mixed up her dates. But it didn't happen: she didn't conceive. As time went on and she was forced to pretend to go to pre-natal appointments she decided that she would have to fake a miscarriage... thank heaven, I was spared that melodrama!'

'Do you think...er...Felicity's having a breakdown?' Lizzie suggested worriedly. 'I mean, maybe it was one of those false pregnancies that come from *genuine* longing for a baby—'

'No.' Maurice Denton's rebuttal was flat, bitter. 'Last night, she informed me that she didn't even like children and that she was fed up not only with the whole insane pretence that she had foisted on us all but also sick and tired of living with a man old enough to be her father! She wasn't even sorry for the damage she did to you, never mind me!'

Lizzie flinched. 'I'm so sorry…'

'Perhaps when a man of fifty-five marries a woman more than thirty years younger he deserves what he gets. Why didn't you come to me about her and the Morgan boy?'

'I…I told myself I couldn't tell you for the baby's sake…but possibly, I just couldn't *face* the responsibility.' Listening to the mayhem of raised voices outside the front door, Lizzie said gently, 'Look, maybe the reporters will go away if I make a statement to them…what do you think?'

'Do as you think best,' Maurice Denton advised heavily. 'Felicity is gone and it can only be Felicity or you that those vultures are interested in. I've never had much of a public profile.'

Lizzie went outside to address the assembled journalist and parry some horrendous questions of the lowest possible taste. 'Was Morgan sleeping with both you and your stepmother?'

'Connor and I were only ever friends,' Lizzie declared with complete calm.

'What about you and Sebasten Contaxis?' she was asked.

'Oh, I'm *not* friends with him!' Lizzie asserted without hesitation and there was a burst of appreciative laughter at that response.

It was only later while she was making a snack for her father that she truly appreciated that her own name had been cleared. Would Sebasten find out? Sooner or later, he would discover that he had targeted the wrong woman. How would he react? But why should she care? What he had confessed to doing was beyond all forgiveness. She looked into the fridge, where a jar of sun-dried tomatoes sat, and her tastebuds watered. Sun-dried tomatoes followed by ice-cream. She shut the fridge again in haste, unnerved by recent food cravings that struck her as bizarre.

An hour later, Sebasten sprang out of his Lamborghini outside the Morgan household in the leafy suburbs. A lingering solitary cameraman took a picture of him. Waving back the bodyguards ready to leap into action and prevent that photo being taken, Sebasten smiled. Sebasten had been smiling ever since he read Patsy Hewitt's hatchet job on Lizzie's stepmother. The wicked stepmother, a typecast figure and a perfect match to Sebasten's own prejudices. He could not imagine how he had contrived not to register that Lizzie's father had a very much younger wife who bore more than a passing resemblance to the evil queen in *Snow White*. He could not imagine how it had not once crossed his mind that Lizzie might be engaged in protecting a member of her own family.

'Lizzie's not friends with you, mate,' the cameraman warned Sebasten.

'Watch this space,' Sebasten advised with all the sizzling, lethal confidence that lay at the heart of his forceful character. He just felt happy, crazy happy, and all he could think about was reclaiming Lizzie.

'She's a gutsy girl…I wouldn't count my chickens.'

Sebasten just laughed and leant on the doorbell and rattled the door knocker for good measure.

CHAPTER TEN

IT WAS very unfortunate for Sebasten that Lizzie had watched his arrival from the safe, shadowy depths of the dining room.

Even at a distance, the slashing brilliance of his smile rocked Lizzie where she stood. He was so gorgeous but that he should *dare* to smile, sure of his welcome, it seemed, before he even saw her, lacerated her pride, fired her resentment and drove home the suspicion that he lacked any sense of remorse. He was tough, ruthless and hard and no relationship with Sebasten would ever go any place where she wanted it to go, she acknowledged with agonised regret. He had already spelt that out in terms no sane woman could ignore.

Hadn't she already got through the first week of being without him? She would get over him eventually, wouldn't she? It dawned on her that on some strange inner level she had not the slightest doubt that Sebasten was about to suggest a reconciliation and that shook her. But once she announced that she had already conceived his child and in addition had every intention of raising that child, Sebasten would surrender any such notion fast. So really, what was she worrying about?

Sebasten had killed his smile by the time Lizzie opened the door. 'Come in…'

'I suggest we go out, so that we can talk,' Sebasten murmured levelly. 'I imagine your family aren't in the mood for visitors today.'

'Only my father is here and he's having a nap in the library.' A quiver assailing her at his proximity, Lizzie pushed wide the door into the drawing room.

'Where's the...' Sebasten bit back the blunt five-letter word brimming on his lips in the very nick of time and substituted, 'your stepmother?'

'Already gone,' Lizzie admitted, tight-mouthed with tension. 'They'll be getting a divorce.'

'Your father's got his head screwed on,' Sebasten asserted with an outstanding absence of sensitivity. 'Booting her straight out the door was the right thing to do.'

'Actually Felicity left under her own steam,' Lizzie declared, making the humiliating connection that she had once been booted out of Sebasten's life with the same efficiency that he was so keen to commend.

'Even better...she won't collect half so much in the divorce settlement,' Sebasten imparted with authority.

'Right at this moment, my father has more to think about than his bank balance!' Lizzie hissed in outrage. 'He's devastated.'

'I was thinking of you, *not* your father. Not very pleasant for you, having to put up with a woman like that in the family,' Sebasten contended, allowing himself to study her taut, pale face, the strain in her unhappy eyes, and then removing his attention again before he was tempted into making the cardinal error of a premature assumption that forgiveness was on the table and dragging her into his arms. 'Why the blazes didn't you spill the beans on your stepmother weeks ago?'

'I believed she was pregnant with my little brother or sister...only it turns out now that she was lying about that to protect herself and keep me quiet.' A tight little laugh fell from Lizzie's lips as she thought of the baby that she carried. It seemed so ironic that the conception which Felicity must initially have been desperate to achieve should have come Lizzie's way instead.

'It sounds like she was off the wall. If it's any consolation, Ingrid Morgan is shattered too and feeling very guilty about the way she treated you,' Sebasten revealed. 'She called me this morning.'

'I don't hold any spite against Connor's mother.' Taut as a bowstring, Lizzie hovered by the window.

'I don't understand why you couldn't tell me the *whole* truth. If you had named your father's wife, I would never have disbelieved your explanation and I could have been trusted with that information.'

Lizzie noted without great surprise that Sebasten was playing hardball and landing her with a share of the blame for *his* refusal to have the smallest faith in her. 'I'm not so sure of that. You and your old friend Ingrid wanted your pound of flesh, regardless of who got hurt in the process!'

Sebasten did not like the morbid tone of that response at all. 'I misjudged you and I'll make it up to you.'

'Was that an apology?'

'*Theo mou*…give me time to get there on my own!' Sebasten urged in a sudden volatile surge that disconcerted her and let her appreciate that he was not quite as cool, calm and collected as he appeared. 'I am sorry, truly, deeply sorry.'

'I can't be,' Lizzie confided shakily.

'I'm not asking *you* to be sorry,' Sebasten pointed out in some bewilderment, wondering whether the shine of tears in her eyes was a promising sign that the very first humble apology he had made to a woman in his entire life had had the right effect.

'You see, I *can't* be sorry that you misjudged me because if I hadn't found that out, I would never have discovered what a ruthless, conscience-free louse you are,' Lizzie completed in a wobbly but driven voice.

Sebasten spread lean brown hands in a natural expression of appeal. 'But I'll never be like that with you again,' he protested. 'I want you back in my life.'

'Oh, I'm sure you'll find another dumb woman to take my place,' Lizzie snapped out brittly and turned her back on him altogether while she fought to rein back the tears threatening her.

'Yes, I could if I wanted to but there's one small problem…I only want *you*.'

In his bed, that was all, Lizzie reflected painfully, her throat thick with tears. She forced herself back round to face him again and tilted her chin. 'I think you'll give up on that ambition when I tell you what I have to tell you.'

'Nothing could make me give up on you,' Sebasten swore, moving forward and reaching for her without warning to tug her forward into his arms.

Lizzie only meant to stay there a second but Sebasten had come to the conclusion that action was likely to be much more effective than words that appeared to be getting him precisely nowhere. He framed her flushed face with two lean hands and gazed down into her distraught green eyes. 'Why are you looking at me like that?' he was moved to demand in reproach. 'I will never hurt you again.'

Trembling all over, Lizzie parted dry lips and muttered, 'I'm pregnant…'

Pregnant? That announcement fell on a male quite unprepared for that kind of news. Sebasten tensed, not even sure he had heard her say what she had just said. 'Pregnant?' he echoed, his hands dropping from her.

'Yes,' Lizzie confirmed chokily.

'Pregnant…' Sebasten said again as though it was a word that had never come his way before and innate caution was already telling him to shut up and not say another single sentence. But he was so shattered by the concept of Lizzie being pregnant that not all the caution in the world could keep him quiet. 'Is it Connor's?' he shot at her rawly, savage jealousy gripping him in an instant vice.

Watching the flare of volatile gold in his stunning eyes, the fierce cast of his superb bone-structure, Lizzie was backing away from him and she only stilled when her shoulders met the china cabinet behind her. 'No, it is not your half-brother's child. Even Connor was not low enough to try to get me into bed while he was making mad, passionate love to my stepmother behind my back. I never slept with Connor,' Lizzie spelt out shakily.

Sebasten recalled his own belief in her inexperience the first night he had shared with her but Sebasten was always stubborn and not quite ready in the state of numb shock he was in to move straight in and embrace the possibility of a child he had never expected to have. 'How do I know that for sure?'

Temper leapt with startling abruptness from the sheer height of Lizzie's tension. 'You're the only lover I've ever had…is it *my* fault you were too busy taking advantage of me to even notice that I was a virgin?'

'I didn't take advantage of you and if you're telling me the truth you're the only virgin I've ever slept with,' Sebasten launched back, playing for time while he mulled over what she had said but all his anger ebbing at miraculous speed. Even so, that did not prevent him from finding another issue. 'You said you were protected.'

'I was sick the next morning…it might have been that or it might just be that I fall into the tiny failure-rate percentage…but the point *is*,' Lizzie framed afresh, 'I am pregnant and it's yours.'

'Mine…' Sebasten was now unusually pale at the very thought of what he saw as the enormous responsibility of a baby. All he had to do was think about his own nightmare childhood, the misery inflicted on him by self-preoccupied adults who left him to the care of unsupervised staff when it suited them and isolated him in boarding schools, where he had also been forgotten with ease. Nobody knew better than he that even great wealth was no protection when it came to a child's needs.

'I appreciate that this is a shock for you,' Lizzie conceded when she could hear that ghastly silence no longer. 'But I should also add that I'm going to *have* this baby—'

Emerging from his unpleasant recollections. Sebasten frowned at her in complete innocence of her meaning. 'What else would you do?'

Silenced by that demand, Lizzie blinked.

'I suppose we'll have to make the best of it,' Sebasten breathed, squaring his broad shoulders in the face of his inner conviction that life as he knew it had just been slaughtered. But much of his gloom lifted on the sudden realisation that, of course, Lizzie would come in tow with the baby. With Lizzie back in his life and him ensuring in a discreet way that the baby was never, ever neglected for even a moment, he could surely rise to the challenge?

'And what would making the best of it…entail?' Lizzie prompted thinly.

'Sebasten expelled his pent-up breath in an impatient hiss. 'Obviously, I'll have to marry you. It's my own fault. I should've taken precautions too that night but we're stuck with the consequences and I'm a Contaxis…not the sort of bastard who tries to shirk his responsibilities!'

During that telling speech, Lizzie almost burst into a rage as big as a bonfire. She went lurching from total shock at the speed with which he mentioned marriage when she had never dreamt he might even whisper that fatal word. Then she truly listened and what she heard inflamed her beyond belief.

'I don't want to marry you—'

'You've got no choice—'

'Watch my lips—I do not *want* to marry you!'

Sebasten dealt her a grim appraisal in which his powerful personality loomed large. 'Of course you do. Right now, we've got a bigger problem than me being a ruthless, conscience-free louse!' he countered with sardonic bite. 'Can we please focus on the baby issue?'

'You don't want to marry me…you don't want the baby either!' Lizzie flung at him in condemnation, feeling as though her heart was breaking inside her and hating him for not being able to feel what she felt.

'I want you and I'll get used to the idea of the baby,' Sebasten declared.

Intending to show him out the front door, Lizzie yanked

the drawing-room door wide and then froze. Her father was standing in the hall, his face a stiff mask of disbelief. It was obvious that he had heard enough to appreciate that she was carrying Sebasten's child. He looked at her with all his disappointment written in his eyes and it was too much to her after the day she had already endured. With a stifled sob, Lizzie fled for the sanctuary of her old apartment in the stable block.

Sebasten could see 'potential ally' writ large in his future father-in-law's horror at the revelation that his unmarried daughter was expecting a baby. 'I'm sorry you had to hear the news like that. Naturally, Lizzie's upset by the circumstances but I'm just keen to get the wedding organised.'

Maurice Denton was relieved by that forthright declaration. Unfreezing, almost grateful for a distraction from his own personal crisis, he offered Sebasten a drink. Sebasten accepted the offer.

He had never been more on edge: he felt as if Lizzie was playing games with him and that was not what he expected from her. It took time to concede that he might have been a little too frank about his reactions and that perhaps lying in his teeth would have gone down better. After a third drink to Sebasten's one, Maurice informed Sebasten that should be himself live until he was ninety-nine he had no hope of ever hearing a marriage proposal couched in less attractive terms. He then asked his son-in-law-to-be if he was shy about being romantic.

Sebasten tried not to cringe at the question but he was honest in his response: he had never made a romantic gesture in his entire life.

'I think you'd better get on that learning curve fast,' Lizzie's father advised before going on to entertain Sebasten with stories of how devoted a mother Lizzie had been to her dolls and how much she had always adored fussing round babies.

While the older man began to find some solace not only

in those happier memories of the past but also in the prospect of a grandchild after the humiliation of his own disappointed hopes of another child, Sebasten began to imagine the baby as a miniature version of Lizzie tending to her dolls and relax and even warm to the prospect.

A copy of Lizzie's birth certificate having been supplied helpfully by her parent, Sebasten drove off to apply for a special licence that would enable him to marry Lizzie within the week. Mindful of that galling advice about romance, he went on to pay a visit to a world-famous jewellery store. He chose the most beautiful rare diamond on offer and a matching wedding ring.

Late that evening, Sebasten returned to the Denton household as confident as he had been of his reception earlier in the day, only on this second occasion convinced he was infinitely better prepared to deliver exactly what was expected of him. Lizzie could hardly doubt the strength of his commitment to marrying her when he had already made *all* the arrangements for the wedding on his own.

That afternoon, Lizzie had had a good cry about Sebasten's crass and wounding insensitivity. She had tried hard to respect his honesty but in point of fact it had hurt too much for her to do that. She might love him but there were times when furious frustration and pain totally swallowed up that love. With the best will in the world, how could she marry a guy who didn't want a wife and could only stick children at a distance or inanimate on a painted canvas? No crystal ball was required to foresee the disaster that would result from Sebasten making himself do what he had always sworn he would not do.

Sebasten took the steps up to Lizzie's apartment three at a time. The door wasn't shut and he frowned. It was dangerous to be so careless of personal safety in a big city. She really *did* need him around. He let himself in. Lizzie was curled up on a big, squashy sofa, fast asleep. She was wearing a pale pink silk wrap, another colour to add to the already wide spectrum of shades which Sebasten considered framed Lizzie to perfection. He crouched down by her side.

Lifting up her limp hand, he threaded the engagement ring onto her finger. Now she was labelled *his* for every other man to see. As that awareness dawned on him, Sebasten finally saw the point of engagements. She got the little ring, he got to post the much more important hands-off-she's-mine giant ring of steel. He liked that. This romantic stuff? Easy as falling off a log, Sebasten decided.

With a sleepy sigh, Lizzie opened her eyes and focused on Sebasten and thought she was back in bed with him again, which she very often *was* in her most secret dreams. Enchanted by the pagan gold glitter of his intense gaze, she let appreciative fingers drift up to trace a high, angular cheekbone. He caught her hand in his and captured her lips in a sensual, searching exploration that was an erotic wake-up call to every sense she possessed. She leant up the better to taste him, breathe in the achingly familiar scent that was uniquely his, close her arms round his neck so that she could sink greedy fingers into the depths of his luxuriant black hair.

Sebasten made a low, sexy sound of encouragement deep in his throat. Scooping her up, he sank back with her cradled in his arms and let his tongue dip in a provocative slide between her lips. Lizzie jerked and strained up to him, wanting, needing, possessed by helpless excitement and hunger for more.

'You still want me, *pethi mou*,' Sebasten husked, pausing to trail his mouth in a tantalising caress down the line of her long, elegant neck. 'But I can't stay long. Your father has been very understanding and tolerant but I won't risk causing offence.'

Emerging for the first time since she had wakened to proper awareness, Lizzie snatched in a quivering gasp of shame and embarrassment: she had fallen like an overripe plum into Sebasten's ready hands. 'This shouldn't be happening,' she bit out shakily and flew upright to smooth down her wrap.

Only then did she register the weight of the ring now adorning her hand. In disbelief, she raised her fingers to stare at the fabulous solitaire diamond sparkling in the lamplight.

'Like it?' Sebasten lounged back on the sofa with the indolent, expectant air of a male bracing himself to withstand fawning feminine approbation.

'What is it?'

'You really need to be told?'

Lizzie jerked her chin in an affirmative nod, for she could not credit that the male she had flatly refused to marry could have bought her an engagement ring and what was more put in on her finger without her knowledge or agreement.

'It matches the wedding ring. I got it too.' Well-aware of her shaken silence and proud of that seeming achievement, Sebasten rose to his full height so that she could fling herself at him and hug him.

'You…*did*!' Lizzie parroted, a swelling forming in her tight chest that she did not immediately recognise as rage.

'In fact, I've been extremely busy,' Sebasten extended in his rich dark drawl. 'I've got a special licence. I've got the church booked and a top-flight wedding-planners outfit burning the midnight oil on the finer details even as we speak. You have nothing to do but show up looking gorgeous on Saturday—'

'You mean…I get to pick my own dress?'

'I contacted an Italian designer…they're flying over a team on Wednesday with a selection for you.'

'Oh…*this* Saturday?' Momentarily Lizzie's rage took a back seat to shock at the sheer level of organisation that had taken place behind her back and the news that her own wedding was to be staged in just six days' time.

'Your father agreed that we shouldn't hang around.'

'Did he really?' Lizzie queried in a rather high-pitched

tone. 'Sebasten…cast your mind back to my answer to your declaration that we should marry.'

'You said no but I knew you didn't mean it,' Sebasten informed her.

'D-did you?' Lizzie's response shook with the force of her feelings but she looked again at the ring on her engagement finger. Her eyes stung and she spun away, remembering the guy who had hired decorators to leave her free to dine with him. He did what *he* thought best and if that meant refusing to credit her refusal, using her own father as back-up and going ahead and arranging a wedding all on his own, he was more than equal to the challenge.

And more than anything else in the world she would have loved to have faith in that blazing confidence he wore like an aura and rise to that same challenge. But he didn't love her, was only offering to marry her because she was pregnant and he had *never* wanted a child. Where would they be in a few months' time when she was more in love and more dependent on him than she was even now and he discovered that good intentions were not enough? He wouldn't find her so attractive once her slender figure vanished. He might even be downright repulsed by her fecund shape. He might get bored, he might even stray and she would be destroyed…absolutely, utterly destroyed by such a rejection.

'I can't do it,' Lizzie whispered.

Sebasten linked strong arms round her and slowly turned her round. 'Bridal nerves,' he told her with a determined smile.

'I can't do it,' Lizzie whispered again, white as milk. 'I *can't* marry you.'

Sebasten freed her and took a step back. He was making a real effort to control the stark anger threatening his control but he could not understand what was the matter with her. He had done every single thing he could think of to please her and she had not voiced one word of appreciation. She had not even appeared to register his enthusiasm for something he had never, ever thought he would do.

'The baby *must* have the Contaxis name and my protection,' he spelt out. Eyes dark as the night sky pinned to her taut, trouble face. 'That's not negotiable.'

'Commands don't cut it with me,' Lizzie snapped, feeling the full onslaught of his powerful personality focused on her and rebelling.

'Then tell me what *does* because I sure as hell have no idea!' Sebasten raked back at her in sudden dark fury.

Trembling, Lizzie whirled away again. Although she loved him, she had a deep instinctive need to keep herself safe from further hurt and disillusionment. He had too much power over her, and how could she trust him when only his sense of responsibility had persuaded him to offer marriage? She saw the sense in his insistence that they marry to give their baby his name, for the law as it stood did not recognise less formal relationships. Yet to marry him and live with him as a wife felt like a giant step too far for her at that moment.

If *only* there was something in between, a halfway house that could answer her needs and the baby's without trapping Sebasten into immediate domesticity and commitment before he could judge whether or not he could meet those demands in the long term. A halfway house, she thought in desperation, and then the solution came to her in a positive brainstorm.

'I want an answer,' Sebasten told her fiercely.

A flush on her cheeks, excitement in her eyes, for Lizzie was eager to come up with a blueprint that would allow her to marry him. 'I have it. We don't live together…you buy me a house of my own!'

'Say that again…no, *don't*.' Sebasten warned, studying her with laser-like intensity, shimmering golden eyes locked to her in disbelief.

'But don't you see it? It would be perfect!' Lizzie told

him with an enthusiasm that could only inflame. 'You could visit whenever you liked.'

'Really?' Sebasten's bitten-out response was not quite level while he wondered if she was feeling all right, but he was reluctant to risk asking that question in case she took it as an insult.

'We would each hold on to more of our own separate lives than married couples usually do. You'd have your business and I'd have my new PR job—'

'What new PR job?' Sebasten interrupted faster than the speed of light.

'I'm starting tomorrow—'

'But you're pregnant—'

'Pregnant women work in PR too—'

'You were working for *me*, Sebasten remind her, taking a new tack as his raging frustration rose to almost ungovernable heights. He didn't want her working any place and certainly not in some freewheeling PR firm where she would be engaged in constant interaction with other men and a frantic social life.

'Not any more and it wasn't a good idea, was it? Other people don't feel comfortable working around a woman who may be involved with the boss. So, as I was saying…if we lived in separate houses we wouldn't crowd each other.'

Dark colour now scored Sebasten's rigid cheekbones. 'Maybe I fancied being crowded.'

Lizzie breathed in deep. 'And I think…the first couple of months anyway…you shouldn't stay overnight.'

'I can tell you right now upfront that I won't buy a separate house and either you take me overnight or you take me not at all!' Sebasten launched at her with savage incredulity.

Lizzie swallowed the thickness of tears clogging her throat. 'You can't blame me for trying to protect myself. I don't want to be hurt again and it's going to take time for me to be able to trust you.'

Sebasten spread rigid hands and clenched them into tight, angry fists in silence. So it was payback time. Oh, yes, he understood that. She wanted to put him through hell to punish him and it would be a cold day in hell before he accepted humiliation from any woman!

'You're taking this the wrong way,' Lizzie said anxiously.

'I don't like being taken for a ride—'

'I just want us both to have the space and the freedom to see whether or not we want to live together—'

'I know that now...what is the matter with *you*?' Sebasten demanded rawly.

'I won't agree to any other arrangement before Saturday,' Lizzie countered shakily, crossing two sets of fingers superstitiously behind her back and offering up a silent prayer.

A sexless, endless probation period during which she made him jump through hoops like a wild animal being trained? Sebasten could barely repress a shudder.

'Forget it...' he advised between clenched teeth, outraged, stormy dark eyes unyielding.

The silence lay thick and heavy and full of rampant undertones of aggression.

'Is it...well, is it the lack of sex that makes this idea of mine so unacceptable?' Lizzie finally prompted awkwardly.

'Where would you get a weird idea like that?'

'OK...sex is included,' Lizzie conceded, reddening to her hairline at her own dreadful weakness in failing to stand firm.

So he would buy her a house which she would never, never live in, Sebasten reflected, sudden amusement racing through him at the speed with which she had removed the ban on intimacy.

'I suppose it might be rather like keeping a mistress,' Sebasten mused, watching her squirm at that lowering concept with immense satisfaction. 'OK…it's a deal. I'll go for it.'

But when Sebasten climbed into his car minutes later, neither satisfaction nor amusement coloured his brooding thoughts. She didn't love him. If she had ever loved him, he had killed that love. She would accept the security of marriage but she was set on having a separate life. Yet he had always been separated from other people, initially by wealth and being an only child, later by personal choice, when keeping his relationships at an undemanding superficial level had become a habit.

Yet somewhere deep down inside him Sebasten registered that he had had a dream of living a very different life with Lizzie, Lizzie *and* the baby. A life where everything was shared. He did not know when that had started or even how it had developed and that such a dream even existed shook and embarrassed him. Especially after his bride-to-be had spelt out *her* dream of two separate households, talked about space and freedom and only included her body as a last-resort sop to his apparent weak masculine inability to get by without sex.

Intellect told him that he would be insane to accept such terms.

Only a guy who was plain stupid would accept such terms.

Or a guy who was…desperate?

At supersonic speed, Sebasten reminded himself that their main objective was taking care of their future child's needs and that it was better not to dwell on inconsequentials.

CHAPTER ELEVEN

LIZZIE discovered the hard way that embarking on her first career job the same week she planned to get married was a very great challenge.

On the balance side, she thrived in a more informal working environment where a designer-clad appearance was a decided advantage and she was earning almost twice the salary she had earned at CI. She got on great with her new colleagues, was immediately given sole responsibility for organising a celebrity party for the opening of a new nightclub and spent the entire week wishing there were more hours in the day.

Having to slot in choosing her entire bridal trousseau in the space of one extended lunch hour, however, annoyed her. Spending two evenings drumming up interest in the new club by frantic socialising with acquaintances now all too keen to be seen in the company of the future wife of Sebasten Contaxis was even worse. Being pregnant also seemed to mean that she tired much more easily and she just paled when she thought of how difficult it would be to fit ante-natal appointments into such action-packed extended work hours.

She thought about Sebasten with a constant nagging anxiety that kept her awake at night when she most needed to sleep. He spent the first half of the week away on a business trip, and although he called her he seemed rather distant. She asked herself what more she had expected from him. What had seemed in the heat of the moment to be the perfect solution to her concerns about marrying him now seemed more and more like a mistake.

What real chance was she giving their marriage or

Sebasten by insisting on separate accommodation? What true closeness could they hope to achieve if they lived apart? It was also much more likely that, shorn of any perceptible change in his life, Sebasten would continue to think of himself as single. That was hardly a conviction she wanted to encourage. And, in telling him upfront that she didn't trust him and yammering about space and freedom, wasn't she giving him the impression that he would be wasting his time even *trying* to adapt to the concept of a normal marriage?

In the light of those unsettling second thoughts on the issue, Lizzie's heart just sank when Sebasten phoned her forty-eight hours before their wedding to announce that he had found the perfect house for her requirements.

'Gosh, that was quick!' was all she could think to say in an effort to conceal her dismay at the news.

Lizzie had not seen Sebasten since the night they agreed to marry. Yet when he picked her up that evening to take her to view the house, he proved resistant to her every subtle indication that she was just dying to be grabbed and held and kissed senseless. After a week in which she had missed him every hour of every day, one glimpse of his lean, devastatingly handsome features and lithe, powerful frame and she was reduced to a positive pushover of melting appreciation.

'I really love my ring,' she told him encouragingly. 'And the wedding planners you hired are just fantastic.'

'I didn't want you overdoing things when you were pregnant. How's the PR world shaping up?'

'It's demanding but a lot of fun,' she said with rather forced cheer, not adding that after only four days she had reached the conclusion that it was the perfect career for a single woman without either a husband or children.

'You'll be able to rest round the clock on our honeymoon,' Sebasten informed her drily.

'*What* honeymoon?' Lizzie gasped. 'A week into the job, I can't ask for time off!'

'Then it's just as well I asked for you. Your boss was very accommodating—'

'He was…?'

'Naturally. You're an enormous asset to the firm. As my wife, you will have unparalleled access to the cream of society and the kind of contacts most PR companies can only dream about. You could dictate your own working hours, even go part-time.' Sebasten dropped that bait in the water and waited in hope of hearing it hooked.

'Quite a turnaround from my working conditions at Contaxis International,' Lizzie could not resist remarking while cringing with shame at the reality that she had almost leapt on that reference to part-time work. Wouldn't he be impressed if she took that easy way out at such speed?

His strong profile tensed. 'Blame me for that. I wanted the spoilt little rich girl to learn what it was like to have to work for a living. Yet I would never have been attracted to you had you been what I believed you were.'

The Georgian town house he took her to see was only round the corner from his own London home and Lizzie did not comment on that reality when he did not, but her heart swelled with hope at the proximity he seemed keen to embrace. It was a lovely house, modernised with style and in wonderful decorative order. His lawyers, he explained, had negotiated a compensation agreement with the current tenants, who were prepared to vacate the house immediately. In a similar way, the owner had made a very substantial profit from agreeing to sell quickly.

'You always get what you want, don't you?' Lizzie muttered helplessly, struggling to admire the elegant, spacious rooms but increasingly chilled at the prospect of living there alone. She must have been crazy to demand such an eccentric lifestyle, she decided, close to panic. Feeling horribly guilty and confused by her own contrariness, she talked with gushing enthusiasm about how much she was looking forward to moving in.

Sebasten had been on keen watch for withdrawal pangs from the separate-house commitment. After all, the house would be a bit large perhaps but perfect in every other way for his future father-in-law, who had already mentioned a desire to sell the home he had shared with his estranged wife. As Lizzie complimented all that she saw, his hopes that she might never move into the house suffered a severe setback.

On her wedding day, Lizzie donned a gown fit for a fairy tale. The exquisite beaded, embroidered bodice bared her smooth shoulders and the flowing full skirt made the utmost of her tall, slender figure.

Surprise after wonderful surprise filled her day. A gorgeous sapphire and diamond necklace and earrings arrived from Sebasten as well as a blue velvet garter for good luck. Although she had never indicated any preference for certain flowers, her bouquet was a classic arrangement of her favourites. The equivalent of Cinderella's coach drawn by white horses came to ferry her the short distance to the church. Seeing everywhere the evidence of Sebasten's desire to make their wedding match her every possible fantasy, she was a radiant bride.

Her heart swelled when she walked down the aisle and Sebasten turned to watch her with a breathtaking smile on his lean dark features. Surely no guy marrying against his own will could manage a smile that brilliant? Hugging that belief to herself, she cherished every moment of the ceremony and sparkled with quicksilver energy in the photos taken afterwards.

'You look stunning,' Sebasten groaned in the limo that whisked them away from the church and, tugging her close, he ravished her soft raspberry-tinted mouth under his, awakening such a blaze of instant hunger in Lizzie that she clung to him.

'I'm wrecking your lipstick...your hair,' Sebasten

sighed, setting her back from him with hands that he couldn't keep quite steady.

Loving his passion, Lizzie awarded him a provocative look of appreciation. 'It was worth it.'

There was an enormous number of guests at the reception. Introductions and polite conversations continually divided her and Sebasten and it was a relief for Lizzie to glide round the dance floor in the circle of his arms, safe from such interruptions.

'I feel awful…I just can't feel the same about friends who dropped me after Connor's death because of those stupid rumours,' Lizzie confided ruefully.

Sebasten stiffened, realising he disliked even the sound of his half-brother's name on her lips and discomfited by the discovery. 'Are there guests here who did that to you?'

'Loads of them. A good half of them I've known since I was a kid, and Dad's acquainted with their families too, so I didn't feel I had the option of leaving them off the guest list.'

'I wouldn't have given *one* of them an invite!' Shimmering dark golden eyes pinned to her in clear reproof. 'You're too soft. If someone crosses me once, they don't get a second chance.'

Lizzie tensed. 'Didn't I cross you too?'

Sebasten wrapped her even closer to his big, powerful frame, infuriated by the knowledge that she had been snubbed and ignored by people she had considered to be her friends and then been so forgiving. 'Continually…but then you inhabit a very special category, *pethi mou*.'

Lizzie looked up at him with her irreverent grin. 'Remind yourself of that the next time I cross you…you know,' she added impulsively, 'if I look very hard I can see that you *do* bear a slight resemblance to Connor.'

Taken aback by that sudden assurance, Sebasten's superb bone-structure tensed. 'Why are you even looking for a resemblance?'

At the coolness of that demand, Lizzie coloured in surprise. 'Only because you told me that you were half-brothers...and there is only a vague similarity. In your height and build, around the eyes, that's all.'

Without the smallest warning, Sebasten found himself wondering whether she had been drawn to him in the first instance because he reminded her of his younger brother. Until that same moment, he had not actually thought through what he had finally learned about his half-brother's relationship with Lizzie. Connor had cheated on her with another woman, Connor had essentially done the rejecting and wasn't it possible that Lizzie had been left carrying a torch?

'What's wrong?' Lizzie asked because Sebasten had fallen still in the middle of the dance.

'I should've warned you that Connor's true parentage is a secret. Ingrid had her own good reasons for successfully fooling my father into believing that Connor was another man's child. Connor himself never knew the truth.' His lean dark features were taut. 'Nor does his mother want it known even now.'

'I haven't mentioned it to anyone,' Lizzie swore, assuming that fear of her having already been indiscreet had roused his concern on Ingrid Morgan's behalf. 'To be frank, after what I had to put up with on his and Felicity's behalf, he wouldn't be my favourite conversational topic.'

Although Connor was most definitely not Sebasten's favourite topic either, Sebasten discovered that his thoughts continued to circle back in that direction. He sacked his memory in an effort to recall every word that Lizzie had said the night he took her out to dinner and she told him her side of the story on Connor. But he hadn't been listening, not the way he *should* have been listening, for at that point he had believed that her every word was a lie.

'So you can finally tell me where we're going for our honeymoon?' Lizzie carolled with rather contrived sparkle when they boarded his private jet some hours later.

'Greece.' Sebasten reflected that there had to be some

evil fate at work, for he was taking her to the one place in the world that held once fond memories of Ingrid and Connor.

Still striving gamely not to react to his brooding aura, Lizzie smiled so wide her jaw ached. 'You're taking me to your home there?'

'A private island.' Not the brightest spark of inspiration he had had this century, Sebasten decided with grim irony.

'Whose island?'

'Mine.'

'You own your own island?'

'Doesn't every Greek tycoon?' Sebasten shrugged.

'So I'm being dead vulgar and I'm impressed!' Lizzie quipped, a glint of annoyance flaring in her green eyes.

They had enjoyed the most fabulous wedding. Sebasten had seemed to be in the best of humour and nothing had gone wrong that she knew of. So what was the matter with him? Was it only now sinking in on him that he was a married man? Was being married to her *that* depressing? Tears prickled at the backs of her eyes but her expressive mouth tightened and she lifted a magazine, enjoyed the superb meal she was served and said not another word.

Late evening, they arrived on the island of Isvos. The helicopter set them down within yards of a long, low, rambling house built of natural stone. Sebasten carried her over the threshold. 'Bet you're glad there isn't a flight of steps!' Lizzie giggled.

His brilliant gaze centred on her lovely laughing face and suddenly he smiled.

The interior enchanted Lizzie: polished terracotta floors, stone walls and rough-hewn support pillars of wood contrasted with glorious sheer draperies and pale contemporary furniture. In every main room, doors opened direct on to the beach and the whispering, soothing sound of the surf seemed to flow through the whole house.

'I love it,' Lizzie murmured with an appreciative smile. 'It's so peaceful.'

'Ingrid Morgan helped to design it.'

Lizzie glanced at him in surprise. 'I thought she used to be a very superior PA.'

'She was but she was also my father's mistress.'

Lizzie blinked and then her lush mouth rounded into a soft silent 'oh' of belated comprehension.

'She ended it before Connor got old enough to suspect the truth and moved back to England.'

'Has she ever come back here?' Lizzie asked.

'No. Ingrid's not into reliving the past.' His jacket cast on the chest at the foot of the handsome beech bed, Sebasten lounged back against the pale wood door frame, six feet four inches of glorious leashed male power and virility. 'Neither am I as a rule. But, as I'm sure you'll recognise, Connor is a subject we've never really discussed in any depth.'

'Connor…?' Lizzie repeated after a startled pause. 'You want me to talk about Connor…*in depth*?'

Lean, powerful face taut with determination, Sebasten shifted a broad shoulder in a fluid movement. 'We should get it out of the way.'

'Well, excuse me…' Green eyes wide with annoyance and discomfiture, Lizzie tilted her chin. 'I wasn't aware there *was* anything to get out of the way!'

'I know next to nothing about your relationship with him,' Sebasten countered with immovable cool.

'This is our wedding night and you want me to rehash unpleasant memories of another man…is that right?' Lizzie demanded, snatching in a sustaining breath in an effort to control the incredulous resentment splintering through her but failing. 'Go take a hike, Sebasten!'

Sebasten straightened, beautiful dark eyes flaring stormy gold. 'I might just do that.'

At that threat, fear touched Lizzie deep and that very fear that he might walk out only increased her fury. 'Wasn't it bad enough that you spent most of the trip here hardly speaking to me? I put up with that but I can't stand moody people. You never know where you are with them—'

'I am not moody,' Sebasten grated in an electrifying undertone. 'But when you admitted that you saw a likeness between me and Connor, yes, it did give me pause for thought. It made me wonder just what you *first* saw in me...'

Understanding came to Lizzie and she studied him with angry, hurt condemnation, for she could not change the reality that she had met his brother first. 'You have to be the most possessive guy I've ever met—'

Sebasten shot her a fulminating look. 'I'm not and I have never been possessive—'

'Volatile...possessive...jealous. Pick any one of them and they every one fit! If I'd just popped out of a little locked box somewhere the first night we met, you'd have loved it! How *could* you ask about Connor tonight of all nights? Do you honestly think I want to talk about how I found him and my stepmother in bed together?' Lizzie slung at him in furious reproach. 'You haven't got a romantic, sensitive bone in your body!'

The bathroom door slammed and locked on Lizzie's impassioned exit. Sebasten strode out onto the beach, angry with her, angry with himself, angrier still with Connor, now that he finally knew how brutal an awakening she had had to that affair. But he was not volatile. Nobody had ever accused him of that before. He was a very self-controlled guy. As for being possessive, what was wrong with that? *Theo mou*...she was his *wife*! A certain amount of possessiveness was a natural male instinct. As for that other tag, he wouldn't even dignify that suggestion with consideration.

Lizzie's frustration was overborne by tears of sheer tiredness. Where did Sebasten get the energy to be so volatile? At least though she now understood what had been riding him since the reception. She should never have mentioned that bit about there being a resemblance between him and his half-brother. She sank down on top of the comfortable bed, thinking that in just a moment she would go and track Sebasten down and smooth things over. After all, it was kind of sweet: Connor couldn't have held a candle to Sebasten in looks, personality or desirability.

When Sebasten strolled back in off the beach half an hour later, Lizzie was sound asleep. Clad in something filmy the colour of rich honey, she was curled up on top of the shot-silk spread. When he saw the faint track of a tear stain on her cheek, he suppressed a groan and raked long brown fingers through his tousled black hair. Why did he go off the rails with Lizzie? Connor had caused her a lot of grief. On the same score, his own conscience was hardly whiter than white *and* she was carrying his baby…

Lizzie wakened with a start and sat up. The doors on to the beach were still wide but now framed a spectacular crimson and gold sunrise over the bay. The indented pillow beside hers indicated that at some stage of the night Sebasten had joined her and she groaned out loud: she must have slept like a log. Sliding out of bed, she went into the *en suite* bathroom to freshen up and wondered where the heck Sebasten was.

When she returned to the bedroom, she stilled in relief. Sebasten was sprawled on the floor cushion by the doors watching the sun rise and her mouth ran dry. His strong brown back was bare and his well-worn jeans outlined every line of his narrow hips and long, powerful thighs. When he turned his arrogant dark head to look at her, deceptively sleepy golden eyes accentuated by the darkness of his lashes, he just took her breath away.

'Hi…' he said softly, extending a lean hand to her in welcome.

'You should've woken me up last night—'

Sebasten tugged her down beside him and pulled her back against him. 'Be honest…you were exhausted. A siren wouldn't have wakened you—'

'But *you* could have,' Lizzie whispered, curving back

into the sun-warmed heat of him and tightening his arms round her for herself.

'Call it the first selfless act of a lifetime *pethi mou*,' Sebasten teased huskily, brushing her tumbled hair from one slim shoulder and pressing his expert mouth to her exposed skin in a caress that sent a helpless shiver of response coursing through her.

She twisted round in a sudden movement that took him by surprise and locked her lush lips to his with a hunger she couldn't hide.

'And this is the *second* unselfish act...' Sebasten shared with a ragged edge to his dark, deep drawl as he lifted her and set her back from him. 'Breakfast awaits you...'

'B-breakfast?' Lizzie stammered in total disconcertion.

'You can have me for dessert if you want,' Sebasten promised with husky amusement, vaulting upright with easy grace and pulling her with him to walk her out onto the terrace, where fresh rolls, cereal and fruit were already laid on the table.

'Are the staff invisible?' Lizzie asked as he tugged out a seat and tucked her into it.

'I made it. The staff will be very discreet and only show up when necessary—'

'And where do they hang out the rest of the time?'

'In the main house across that hill.' Sebasten nodded in the direction of the thick pine grove that ran on steep sloping ground right down to the edge of the sea.

'There's *another* house?'

'This place wasn't impressive enough to satisfy my father's wives. I use the main house when I'm entertaining. When I'm on my own, I come here.'

That he had brought her with him made her smile. When she had finished her tea, he peeled a peach for her, fed her with it segment by segment. She collided dizzily with smouldering golden eyes and licked his fingers clean of the peach juice. He closed his hands over hers and tugged her upright.

'Ready and willing,' Sebasten husked.

The well-worn denim of his jeans made that so obvious that her cheeks burned with colour but her awareness of his rampant arousal only heightened her own. Driven by the taut sensitivity of her breasts and the ache stirring at the very heart of her, she pushed into connection with every hard, muscular angle of his lean, powerful frame. He knotted his fingers into the tumbling torrent of her hair and claimed her ready mouth with explicit passion.

'I make a really *mean* breakfast,' he teased as he swept her quivering body up into his arms and carried her back to bed.

'But can you do it…every morning?' Lizzie mumbled, trying to hold her own in the breathless dialogue while struggling with his zip.

'Try me…' Sebasten took care of that problem for her by ripping off his jeans with single-minded purpose and dexterity. 'You wouldn't believe how sexy it feels to know that your woman carries your baby inside her.'

'Honestly?' Lizzie opened wide, uncertain eyes, met the fiery confirmation in his intent gaze, and relief and appreciation filled her.

'Honestly,' Sebasten confirmed with the slashing charismatic smile that always made her heart lurch inside her and he deprived her of her nightdress with smooth expertise.

Empowered by that declaration, Lizzie began, 'About last night, what you said about Con—'

'Shut up,' Sebasten warned without the smallest dip in that blazing smile. 'I was way out of line—'

'*But*—'

'Close your eyes and pretend we have only just arrived,' he urged, finding the tender peak of her breast with caressing fingers and depriving her of both breath and concentration.

He took her into a sensual world where all that mattered was the next sweet, drugging high of sensation. He let the heat of his mouth trail over her tender, pouting flesh and a long sigh was driven from her lungs. He lingered over the distended little buds until her sigh had become a moan she wasn't even aware of making and she was shifting her hips in a restive movement, unable to stay still.

'Sebasten…' she gasped as he worked his erotic passage down over the quivering muscles of her tummy. 'I want you…'

'Not yet,' he asserted, parting her slender thighs with ease and embarking on an intimacy that was new to her.

Shaken as she was, her eyes flew wide. 'No…'

But he transformed her negative into a helpless positive within seconds and drove her crazy with a pleasure that came close to torment. She was out of control, abandoned to the urgent need he had driven to an ever greater height. At the instant that her heart was a hammering thunder-beat in her ears and her whole quivering body was sensitised to an almost unbearable degree, he came over her and entered her in a single smooth-driving thrust. Excitement flung her so high, she couldn't catch her breath. She lifted herself up to him, moved against him in a helpless frenzy of need and then cried out as the shock waves of climax took her to an ecstatic peak and then released her again.

She felt soft with love, weak with fulfilment. Revelling in the peaceful aftermath of passion, she rubbed her cheek against a satin-smooth muscular brown shoulder. Happiness cocooned her as he hugged her close. He might not love her but he was very affectionate, she acknowledged, suppressing the inner sense of loss that that first acknowledgement threatened.

'Just to think, *pethi mou*,' Sebasten murmured with raw satisfaction as he gazed down into her warm green eyes, 'nobody but me is ever going to know how fantastic you really are.'

'Trust you to find a new slant on marriage,' Lizzie whispered with amusement.

Dark golden eyes welded to her, he brushed a kiss across

her lush reddened mouth and breathed rather like a guy steeling himself to make a major statement. 'What we have is special…*really* special.'

'Is it?' she muttered, wanting more, striving to silence that need inside her and be happy with what they had.

'Yes.' Sebasten was just a little annoyed that she seemed so indifferent to his attempt to impress on her how much he valued her. 'We're so close, I can *feel* it.'

'Oh…' Lizzie snuggled into him.

'I've never been that great at getting close to women,' Sebasten confided, soothed by the fact that she was now wrapped round him like a vine. 'But you're different. You're very open.'

'Have you ever been in love?' she muttered in as casual a tone as she could muster.

Sebasten tensed. 'No…'

And with that Lizzie had to be content.

Two weeks later, Lizzie shimmied into a dress the shade of copper and noted how well it became the very slight tan she had acquired in the heat of the Greek sun.

Emerald drop earrings dangled from her ears and an emerald and diamond necklace encircled her throat. Sebasten had given her the earrings at the end of the first week and the necklace just the night before. Lizzie smiled. She had never been so happy. Even the reality that her beautiful dress was just a tinge too neat in fit over breasts that had made an inconvenient gain in size as her body changed with early pregnancy couldn't cloud her good mood.

They had had lazy golden days on the beach, eating when they felt like it, swimming when they felt like it, staying in bed when they felt like it and talking long into the night over the exquisite dinners the staff served on the terrace in the evening. On a couple of occasions they had walked down to the sleepy little village at the harbour and dined in each of the two taverns, where they had been treated like guests of honour. Other days they had flown over to the bigger, busier islands like Corfu to shop or dine or dance.

She had learnt a lot about the male she married. She had also been both disconcerted and touched when he had said he would be cutting back on his trips abroad so that he would be able to spend more time with her and the baby.

'It'll be difficult for you,' she had remarked.

'It's my choice, just as it was my father's choice to be a stranger to me throughout my childhood. He was never there,' Sebasten had admitted, his strong jawline squaring as he voiced a truth that his sense of family loyalty had always forced him to repress. 'He expected his wives to do his job for him but they didn't. It was much easier to leave me in the care of the staff or pack me off to boarding school.'

For the first time, Lizzie had recognised the strength of his sense of responsibility towards their unborn baby and her heart had gone out to him as she understood that his own experiences had made him all the more determined to ensure that his own child would receive very different treatment. But for the early loss of her mother, her own childhood had been secure and loving and she began to grasp the source of Sebasten's innate complexity. He had been forced to depend on his own inner resources at too early an age.

Yet throughout those two glorious weeks they shared, Sebasten continually surprised and delighted her with the unexpected. The night that he found her eating sun-dried tomatoes with a fork direct from the jar she had brought out to Greece with her, he had laughed at her embarrassment over her secret craving and carried both jar and her back to bed. But within twenty-four hours a ready supply of Greek sun-dried tomatoes had been flown in.

'It's a Greek baby,' he had pointed out cheerfully.

She would never have dreamt of telling Sebasten but

she truly believed he was a perfect husband. He was romantic, although without ever seeming to realise that he was being romantic. He was also incredibly passionate and tender as well as being the most entertaining male she had ever been with. In short, he was just wonderful. She could not credit that she had been so worried that he might not be ready for the commitment of marriage. She was convinced that at any moment he would open the subject of their living in separate houses when they returned to London and talk her out of what she had already decided had been a very stupid idea.

It was the last night of their honeymoon. Sebasten had selected it as the night they would cast off their newly married seclusion and host a party at the big white villa over the hill. He wanted to entertain all the Greek friends and business acquaintances who had not been able to make it to a wedding staged at such short notice.

'You look fantastic in that dress,' Sebasten informed her as he entered the bedroom.

Lizzie encountered the appreciative gleam in his gaze and just grinned. 'You picked it. The emeralds look spectacular with it too. Thank you.'

'Gratitude not required. Those emeralds accentuate your eyes and I had to have them, *pethi mou.*'

She looked so happy, Sebasten thought with a powerful sense of achievement and satisfaction. He could not believe that she would insist on living apart from him when they got back home again. If she had begun to care for him even a little again, she would surely change her mind.

'How did you get so friendly with Ingrid Morgan?' Lizzie asked as she kicked off her shoes to walk barefoot across the sand. The path that led up through the pine wood to the main house was on the other side of the beach. 'You never did explain that.'

'Between the ages of eight and eleven, I spent every vacation here with Ingrid and Connor. My father would just fly in for a few days here and there,' Sebasten explained wryly.

'*Every* vacation?' Lizzie queried in surprise.

'It suited Andros. He was between wives. Ingrid treated me the same way she treated Connor and I began to think of them as my family.' Sebasten grimaced as if to invite her scorn of such a weakness on his part. 'It ended the day I asked my father when he and Ingrid were getting married.'

'Was marriage so out of the question?'

'By that stage they had already had a stormy on-and-off relationship that spanned quite a few years. He never thought of her as anything other than a mistress and he'd convinced himself that I was too young to ask awkward questions. But he took me back to our home in Athens that same evening and I was an adult before I met Ingrid again.'

'That was so cruel!' Lizzie groaned.

No longer did she wonder why he had once admitted to not trusting her sex, for he had been let down by the only two women he had learned to love when he was a child. His mother had walked away through her own personal choice but Ingrid Morgan had had no choice, for she had had no rights over her lover's son.

Why the hell had he told her all that? Sebasten asked himself in strong exasperation. Lizzie's eyes were glistening with tears and, even as he was warmed by her emotional response on his behalf, he was embarrassed by it too.

Ahead of them lay the big, opulent white villa built by Andros Contaxis for his second wife. Lizzie had had a lengthy tour of the house the week before. While a hugely impressive dwelling with as many rooms as a hotel, it lacked character and appeal. Considering that problem and keen to change the subject to one less sensitive, she murmured in a bright upbeat tone, 'I've got so many plans for the house. I can hardly wait to get home to make a start.

I really will need the advice of a good interior designer, maybe even an architect.'

Sebasten absorbed that admission in angry, startled bewilderment. He assumed she was referring to the house he had offered her for her own sole occupation in London. How the hell could she exude such enthusiasm for literally throwing him back out of her life again? Had nothing that they had shared in recent days made her reappraise that ambition? What was he? A negotiable part of the old sun, sea and sex vacation aboard? Or just a rebound affair after Connor that was now leading to its natural conclusion? Obviously not much more, for all that he was the father of the baby she carried!

Surprised by his silence, Lizzie coloured, for she had assumed that he would be pleased. But then possibly he believed that when they were only just married she had some nerve announcing that she planned to redesign one of his homes. After all, it should have been *his* suggestion, rather than hers, she thought in sudden mortification. Just because her own father had always preferred to let the women in his life take care of such matters did not mean that Sebasten had a similar outlook.

'Of course,' she added hurriedly, striving to backtrack from her stated intention without losing face, 'change doesn't always mean improvement and it could be a mistake to rush into a project that would be so expensive—'

'Spend what you like when you like,' Sebasten delivered in a derisive undertone. 'I couldn't care less.'

Shock sliced through Lizzie. As they entered the villa she stole a shaken glance at his lean, hard profile, wondering what on earth she had said to deserve such a response. Whatever, it was obvious that Sebasten was angry. Furthermore, once their guests began arriving in a flood, Sebasten roved far and wide from her side, leaving her more than once to assume the guise of a faithful follower. He also talked almost exclusively in Greek, which she supposed was understandable when he was mixing with other

Greeks, but on several occasions when she was already aware that their companions spoke English he left her feeling superfluous to their conversations.

'You have all my sympathy,' Candice, a beautiful and elegant brunette, remarked to Lizzie out of the blue.

Having already been informed by Candice that she had once dated Sebasten, Lizzie tensed. 'Why?'

'Sebasten doesn't quite have the look of a male who has taken to marriage like a duck to water.' Exotic dark eyes mocked Lizzie's flush of dismay at that crack. 'But then some men are just born to prefer freedom and it *is* early days yet, isn't it?'

That one stinging comment was sufficient to persuade Lizzie that Sebasten was making a public spectacle of her. Seeing him momentarily alone, she studied him. He looked grim without his social smile, pale beneath his usually vibrant olive skin tone, and concern overcame her annoyance. She hurried over to him and said ruefully, 'Are you going to tell me what's the matter with you?'

'Nothing's the matter.' Hard golden eyes clashed with hers in apparent astonishment.

'But I've hardly seen you this evening—'

'Do we need to stick together like superglue?' Sebasten elevated a sardonic ebony brow. 'I have to confess that after two weeks of round-the-clock togetherness, I'm in need of a breather and looking forward to leading more separate lives when we get home.'

The silence enclosed her like silent thunder.

'Believe me, you're not the only one,' Lizzie breathed, fighting to keep her voice level.

She walked away but inside herself she was tottering in shock and devastation. How could he turn on her like that when she had believed them so close? She loved him to distraction but how could she allow herself to love someone that ruthless in stating his own dissatisfaction with their marriage? What had gone wrong, how it had gone wrong without her noticing seemed unimportant. All that mattered was that once again she herself had been guilty of making a fatal misjudgement about how a man felt about her.

Oh, she knew he didn't love her but she had believed that they were incredibly close for all that. Hadn't he said so himself? But then, what did she believe? What Sebasten said *in* bed or what he said *out* of it? She knew which version her intelligence warned her to place most credence in. She gazed round the crowded room but all the faces were just a blur and the clink of glasses, the chatter and the music seemed distant and subdued. Then, without her even appreciating the fact, the most awful dizziness had taken hold of her. As she lurched in the direction of the nearest seat she was too late to prevent what was already happening, and she folded down on the carpet with a stifled moan of dismay.

Already striding towards her, alerted by her striking pallor and wavering stance, Sebasten was right on the spot to take charge but cool did not distinguish the moments that immediately followed Lizzie's fainting fit. Never an optimist at the best of times, in the guilt-stricken mood he was in, Sebasten was convinced he'd killed her stone-dead and the reality that there were at least three doctors present was of no consolation whatsoever.

Lizzie recovered consciousness to find herself lying on a sofa in another room. Three men were hovering but Sebasten was down on his knees, clutching one of her hands, much as if she were on her deathbed. She blinked, almost smiled as her bemused gaze closed in on his lean, strong face, and then she remembered his words of rejection and what colour she had regained receded again and she turned her head away, sucking in a deep, convulsive breath.

'Only a faint, nothing to really worry about,' Sebasten's best friend from university asserted in bracing Greek. 'A mother-to-be shouldn't be standing for hours on end on such a warm and humid evening—'

'And not without having eaten any supper,' chimed in another friend.

'She has a fragile look about her,' the third doctor remarked, his more pessimistic and cautious nature a perfect match for Sebasten's. 'Entertaining two hundred people tonight may well have been too much for her. This is a warning to you. She needs rest and tender care, and try to keep the stress to a minimum.'

Sebasten was feeling bad enough without the news that his lack of care on almost every possible count had contributed to Lizzie's condition. He scooped her up into his arms. 'I'm taking you up to bed.'

Lizzie made no protest. The more she thought about his rejection, the more anguished she felt, and what self-discipline she had was directed towards thanking the doctors for their assistance and striving to behave normally.

By the time Sebasten had carried Lizzie up to the master-bedroom suite and settled her down on the vast circular bed that had sent her into a fit of giggles when she first saw it, even he was a little out of breath. But so shattered had he been by her collapse and by the gut-wrenching punishment of having been forced to think of what life might be like without her that Sebasten was desperate to dig himself back out of the very deep hole that fierce pride had put him in.

'I was lying in my teeth when I said I was tired of us being together,' Sebasten confessed in a raw, driven undertone.

Thinking that now he felt sorry for her and blamed his own blunt honesty for causing her stupid faint, Lizzie flipped over and presented him with her back. 'I'd like to be on my own.'

'I'm sorry I was such a bastard,' Sebasten framed half under his breath, his dark, deep drawl thick with strain. 'I don't want to score points any more. I *do* want you to be happy—'

'Then go away,' she muttered tightly.

'But I *need* you in my life.' Sebasten forced that admission out with much the same gritty force as a male making a confession while facing a loaded gun.

A solitary tear rolled down Lizzie's taut cheek. Obviously he had recognised just how devastated she was at the concept of having to let go of her dream of a happy, normal marriage. 'I don't need you,' she mumbled flatly.

CHAPTER TWELVE

SEBASTEN had had a hell of a night.

Most of their guests had travelled home. Some who had had to stay overnight at the villa at least retired early, but those who did not kept him up until almost dawn. For what remained of the night he paced the room next to Lizzie's and fought the temptation to disturb her so that they could talk again. While Lizzie breakfasted in bed at his express instruction, he had to assume a cheerful-host act until the merciful moment that the last of their visitors had departed. However, by that stage it was time to embark on their return trip to London.

Lizzie came downstairs dressed in a dark green shift dress, her hair pulled back in a sophisticated style, all but her lush pink lips and the tip of her nose hidden behind a giant pair of sunglasses.

'How do you feel?' Sebasten asked, striving to suppress the recollection of finding her bedroom door locked when he had tried to make the same enquiry earlier in the day.

'Marvellous...can't wait to get home!' Lizzie declared, heading for the helicopter outside at speed.

Behind the sunglasses her reddened eyes were dull with misery but Lizzie had her pride to sustain her. When they boarded the Contaxis jet at Athens, she struck up an animated conversation with the stewardesses, went into several determined fits of laughter at the movie she chose to watch and enjoyed a second dessert after eating a hearty late lunch. And she called *him* insensitive, Sebasten reflected in receipt of that concerted display of indifference.

'I have to call into the office,' Sebasten announced after she had climbed into the limousine waiting to collect them in London. 'I'll see you back at the house...we have to talk.'

But what was there to talk about? Lizzie asked herself wretchedly. He had already spelt out how he felt. She had no option but to go to his London home, for the town house he had purchased had yet to be furnished. So, couldn't she buy some furniture? Surely camping out in bare rooms would be better than staying with Sebasten when her presence was no longer welcome?

How could he get bored with her between one moment and the next? Her throat ached and her rebellious memory served up a dozen images of intimacy that cut her like a knife when she could least bear it. Sebasten dragging her out of bed to breakfast at dawn and enjoy what he called 'the best part of the day' and her struggling to match his vibrant energy and conceal her yawns. Sebasten watching her try on clothes, a smouldering gleam of appreciation in his gaze letting her know exactly what to buy. Sebasten curving her into his arms last thing at night and making her feel so incredibly happy and secure.

No, camping out in bare rooms, she decided with a helpless shiver, would be more comfortable than the chilling prospect of sharing the same household even on a temporary basis, ever conscious of what they had had and then lost. Painful as it was, she knew that some men lost all interest in a woman once the excitement of the chase was over and that those same men could go from desire to uninterest almost overnight. Was that Sebasten's true nature? And had he not already achieved what he had said was most important? Their child would be born a Contaxis. The sad fact was that his parents did not have to live together nor even remain married to meet that requirement.

Infuriated at the crisis that had demanded his presence at Contaxis International, Sebasten got back home just before seven that evening. By then, Lizzie had already cleared out. The dressing room off the master bedroom looked as though a whirlwind by the name of Lizzie had gone through it and his staff had tactfully left the evidence for him to find. She had left a note on the bed. Seeing it, he froze, not wanting to read it.

'I borrowed some of your furniture but I'll return it soon. It's easier this way,' she wrote in her note. 'Stay in touch.'

Stay in touch? Sebasten crunched the note between his fingers. *Easier for whom?* He was in total shock. Nothing he had said the night before had made any impression on her. He had said ' I need you' to a woman who could break down in floods of tears over a sad film, but she had still walked out. Let her go, his stubborn pride urged.

When Sebasten hit the bell on the front door, Lizzie mustered her courage and went to answer it.

Lean, bronzed features taut, he was sheathed in a formal dark business suit. She allowed her gaze to flick over him very fast. He looked sensational, but then he always did, she acknowledged painfully. Heart pounding like a road drill, she crossed the echoing hall and showed him into the only furnished room available.

'Look at me...' Sebasten urged in a roughened undertone.

She was shocked by the haunted strain in his dark gold gaze and the fierce tension stamped into every sculpted line of his hard bone-structure.

'Come home...*please*,' he breathed with fierce emphasis. 'We have to talk.'

'I think that all that needs to be said was said last night,' Lizzie said unevenly.

'No...I tried to give you space while we were in Greece. I went against my own nature.' Sebasten shifted a lean, forceful hand to emphasise that point. 'If I had that two weeks a second time, believe me, I wouldn't make the same mistake again.'

'But you went out of your way to hurt me last night.'

Lizzie's mind was in angry, defensive turmoil, for she could no longer understand what he wanted from her.

Sebasten released a ragged laugh. 'What did you expect from me after I had to listen to you telling me that you couldn't *wait* to start renovating this house? How was I supposed to react? You were letting me know that nothing had changed, that you weren't prepared to live with me or even give our marriage a fighting chance!'

Lizzie stared back at him with wide, bewildered eyes. 'But I wasn't talking about *this* house…I was talking about your father's villa on the island!'

Sebasten stilled in his pacing track across the room and frowned in equal bemusement. 'You didn't make that clear. The villa on Isvos?'

'Yes.' Lizzie took in a slow, steadying breath as she grasped that they had been talking at cross purposes the previous night. His aggression had been fired by a simple misconception: his belief that she was still hell-bent on setting up a separate household. 'You picked me up wrong and leapt to the wrong conclusion.'

'I don't think so.' Sebasten had a different viewpoint. 'You've moved in here.'

'Only because I thought that was what *you* wanted!'

'Why would I want to live apart from my wife?' The fierce glitter in his intent golden eyes challenged her, his jawline clenching hard. 'I thought that I could accept that for a while if it meant that you married me but this feels more like the end of our marriage than the beginning. But I know that I can't force you to feel what I feel.'

'And what *do* you feel?' Lizzie almost whispered, so great was her tension, for what he was telling her was exactly what she had needed to hear from him.

'That maybe you haven't quite got over Connor yet. That maybe this situation is what I asked for when I screwed up our relationship from start to finish…but I still love you and I'll wait for as long as it takes,' Sebasten breathed with fierce conviction.

Lizzie was still as a statue. Shock had made her pale. 'You *love* me?'

Sebasten fixed level, strained golden eyes on her and nodded much as if he had just confessed to a terminal illness.

'Since when?' Lizzie could barely frame the question.

'Probably the first night we met. I did things that night that I would never have done in a normal state of mind,' Sebasten confessed with grim dark eyes, not appearing to register that she was fumbling her way down onto the edge of the sofa she had borrowed. 'I did take *huge* advantage of you. You were very vulnerable that night but I just couldn't let go of you. Love is supposed to make people kinder but at that stage it only made me more selfish and ruthless.'

'Sebasten…' Lizzie was wondering if she could dare to credit what she was hearing when what he was saying was her every dream come true.

'No, I'm determined to tell it like it was, no stone left unturned,' Sebasten asserted with a derision angled at himself. 'After I sobered you up that night, I should've put you in a guest room. On the other hand, if I *had* done that you wouldn't have got pregnant and I could never have persuaded you to marry me. So, I'm afraid I can't even regret that we made love.'

Lizzie could not drag her mesmerised stare from his lean, strong face. 'Yes, he was still very much the focused guy she had fallen in love with. But that he should be grateful that she had conceived because that development had ultimately made her let him back into her life again touched her to the heart.

'And when I suspected that you were a virgin, did I feel guilty?' Sebasten spread rueful hands in emphasis. 'No, I didn't feel guilty even then. That made you feel more like mine, and you're right—where you're concerned I'm very possessive and jealous and I was delighted that I was your first lover.'

'You're being so honest,' Lizzie managed in a shaky voice. 'I really like that.'

'Then I saw your driver's licence and realised you were Lisa Denton and it all just blew up in my face. From there on in, it only got worse,' Sebasten continued heavily.

'The night we met...you *honestly* didn't know who I was?' Lizzie gasped.

'I told you I didn't! I saw you on the dance floor and I couldn't take my eyes off you. I had not the smallest suspicion that you were Connor's ex.'

And she hadn't believed him, Lizzie thought in dismay.

'In fact I thought the little blonde I saw speaking to you was Lisa Denton and I had no intention whatsoever of approaching her.'

'That was Jen,' Lizzie whispered, fully convinced that he was telling her the truth.

'Once I knew your true identity, I couldn't acknowledge how I felt about you. I wrecked everything trying to stay loyal as I believed to Connor's memory.'

'Why, though? You admitted you hardly knew him as an adult.'

Sebasten grimaced. 'The day of the funeral was also the day Ingrid told me that he was my half-brother.'

Lizzie absorbed that fact with a flash of anger in her expressive eyes. 'Oh, that was wicked...to finally tell you *that* when Connor was dead!'

'I wouldn't say it was wicked, but with hindsight I can see that it *was* very manipulative timing,' Sebasten conceded with wry regret. 'But Ingrid was out of her head with grief. It sent me haywire though. I felt a great sense of loss. I felt guilty that I had not made more effort to maintain contact with Connor.'

Lizzie did not believe he would have found very much common ground with his half-brother but she was too kind to say so. Her memory of the younger man had softened but she knew that he had been arrogant and self-centred right to the last in allowing his friends to go on believing that she had broken his heart and driven him to the heavy drinking sessions that finally contributed to his death.

'I've learnt more about Connor through what he did to *you* than I probably ever wanted to know,' Sebasten confided with a grimace, as if he could read her mind. 'What I hate most is that I came along and I hurt you even more.'

'That's behind us now,' Lizzie assured him.

'Time and time again, I told myself that the secret of your incredible attraction was just sex,' Sebasten groaned. 'The minute I realised that you were Lisa Denton, I swore to myself that I wouldn't ever sleep with you again...but I *did* and more than once.'

'I know.' Lizzie was trying hard not to smile.

'That episode in the basement just...' Sebasten threw up both hands in a speaking gesture of rare discomfiture. 'It was crass, crazy. I'm really sorry about that. Afterwards, I couldn't believe I'd lost control to that extent...I mean, I was fighting what I felt for you with everything I had! But I was a pushover every time.'

'That's when you realised how keen I was on you, wasn't it?' Lizzie prompted gently.

Dark colour scored his superb cheekbones. 'I felt like a total bastard and I didn't want to hurt you. So, I decided that I had to dump you because the entire situation had become more than I could handle.'

'You poor love...' Lizzie swallowed hard on the unexpected giggle that bubbled in her throat. 'You've had a really tough time.'

'You dumped me,' Sebasten reminded her. 'I couldn't even do that right!'

Lizzie got up and wrapped her arms round him.

'I thought you were angry with me. Why are you hugging me?' Sebasten asked, his Greek accent very thick.

'For making me feel as irresistible as Cleopatra...for letting me see that loving me has made you suffer a lot too...so now I can forgive you for having made me suffer,' Lizzie confided, locking both arms round his neck.

'You can forgive me?' Some of the raw tension in his big, powerful frame eased and he closed his own arms tightly round her. 'Give me a chance to make everything right from now on?'

'Loads of chances,' she promised, conscious of the anxiety still visible in his dark golden eyes. 'When did you realise you'd fallen in love with me?'

Sebasten tensed. 'I sort of suspected it in Greece but I didn't take those thoughts out and examine them because I didn't know what was going to happen when we came back to London. But when you collapsed last night I panicked and faced how much you meant to me. I had this nightmare vision of my life without you in it—'

'Traumatising? I hope so, because you're not getting a life without me in it.'

'I love you the way I never thought I would love any woman.' His possessive golden gaze pinned with appreciation to her, he framed her irreverent grin with gentle fingers. 'I love everything about you, *pethi mou*…even the way you annoy the hell out of me sometimes. So stop teasing me.'

She could not have doubted the rough sincerity in his every spoken syllable and the direct and steady onslaught of an adoring scrutiny that made her face warm with colour. 'I love you too…'

'*Still?*' Sebasten demanded. 'I thought you'd got over me…you wouldn't give an inch even when I practically begged you to come back to me!'

'I can be stubborn. But I never stopped loving you.'

His brilliant smile flashed across his lean, devastating features and he hugged her close. 'I feel a very uncool degree of happiness…say it again.'

She did.

And then he felt he had to match her with the same words. He felt wonderful. He felt ten feet tall. Lizzie was his, finally, absolutely his. His wedding ring on her finger, his baby on the way. Freeing her just when she was about to invite the kiss that every nerve in her body craved, Sebasten closed his hand over hers and walked her back out to the hall.

'Where are we going?' Lizzie muttered.

'Home…to where it all began. Any chance of me reliving the highlights?' Sebasten gave her a wicked look of all-male anticipation.

As he flipped shut the door in their wake and then tucked her into his car, Lizzie blushed and smiled. 'I think that's very possible.'

An hour and more later, Sebasten lay back in what now felt like a secure marital bed to him and held Lizzie close. He was in a very upbeat mood, checking out her freckles and discovering that, in spite of all his efforts to keep her under sunhats and in the shade, the Greek sun had blessed her with another half-dozen. He knew she wasn't fond of her freckles, so he kept the news to himself. He splayed his fingers over her still non-existent tummy and grinned and secretly rejoiced in feelings of intense possessiveness.

'What are you thinking about?' Lizzie whispered, smiling up at him with complete contentment and trust.

'That you're the best investment I've ever made,' Sebasten confided with quiet satisfaction. 'When you have the baby, I'll have *two* of you.'

'We'll be a family. You'll be totally trapped because I'm not letting go of you ever,' Lizzie teased.

'You'd be amazed how good that sounds to me.' Sebasten looked down at her with all the love he couldn't hide and she knew he meant every word of that assurance. 'As long as you don't expect me to buy any more houses for your sole occupation.'

Lizzie grimaced. 'I feel *so* bad about that.'

'Don't. Just remind yourself that we are the same two people who shared an incredible happy honeymoon and we talked about everything under the sun *but*…neither one of us had the guts to broach the sensitive subject of how we planned to live when we got home again,' Sebasten pointed out with wry amusement.

'I was waiting for you to try and persuade me to change my mind,' Lizzie complained. 'I wasn't expecting you to rush out and buy a house overnight either!'

Sebasten burst out laughing at that and kissed her breathless, and it was another hour before they had dinner and he dropped the bait about it having just occurred to him that perhaps her father might like to consider moving into the surplus dwelling they had acquired.

'That's a *fabulous* idea!' Lizzie exclaimed.

And Sebasten basked without conscience in her pleasure and admiration and knew that he would never own up to the truth that he had hoped for that conclusion all along.

A year and four months later, Sebasten and Lizzie threw a party to celebrate their baby daughter, Gemma's, christening.

Ingrid Morgan attended and Lizzie and she talked at some length. They had made peace with each other months before: Ingrid had felt very guilty and had urged that meeting, but Lizzie had made the effort initially only for Sebasten's sake. However, when she had got to know the older woman better she had begun to relax and like Ingrid for herself. Ingrid had worked through her grief and admitted that she had had no cause to accuse any woman of driving her son to suicide. She had come to terms with the reality that Connor's death had just been an accident.

When all their guests had gone home, Lizzie changed Gemma into her cute bunny nightwear and laid her daughter with tender hands into her cot. She just adored the baby. Gemma had her father's colouring but was already showing signs of her mother's personality. She was a cheerful baby, who slept a lot and rarely cried. Elbows resting on the cot rail, Lizzie smiled down at Gemma, grateful that her baby girl had not inherited her freckles. It was all very well for Sebasten to have a positive *thing* about freckles but he had to appreciate that not everyone shared that outlook, Lizzie reflected with amusement.

It had been an eventful year for both her and her father. Maurice Denton was already divorced. Felicity had met another man and had been keen to speed up the legal proceedings. Her father's spirits had been low for quite a time but moving house had helped and he very much liked living so close to his daughter and was a regular visitor. His own friends had rallied round him in a very supportive way, but her father had also developed a wonderfully friendly and relaxed relationship with Sebasten.

At times during her pregnancy that closeness between her parent and her husband had been just a little irritating for Lizzie. Both Sebasten and her father had been prone to trying to gang up on her and wrap her up in cotton wool. Stubborn to the last, Lizzie had worked until she was seven months pregnant before deciding to tender her resignation. The PR job had been a lot of fun but it had taken her away from Sebasten too many evenings and it had exhausted her.

Gemma had been born without any fuss or complications but Sebasten had lived on his nerves for the last weeks of Lizzie's pregnancy, striving valiantly to conceal his terror that something might go wrong. But Lizzie herself had been an oasis of calm, secure in the knowledge that Sebasten was doing all her worrying for her. He had fallen instantly in love with Gemma and, if possible, Lizzie had fallen even more deeply in love with Sebasten just watching him with their daughter. The guy who had said he preferred children at a distance used every excuse that had ever been invented to lift his daughter and cuddle her.

'Don't you dare lift her,' Lizzie warned, hearing and recognising the footsteps behind her. 'She shouldn't be disturbed when she's ready to go to sleep.'

Sebasten strolled into view, and at one glimpse of his heartbreaking smile Lizzie's pulses speeded up.

'Just when did you get so bossy?' he mocked, brilliant

golden eyes roaming over the very tempting vision Lizzie made in her sleek blue skirt suit with her glorious hair tumbling round her shoulders in sexy disarray.

Lizzie grinned. 'When I met you. Either I lay down and got walked on or I fought back.'

'But you're out of line on this occasion. I spent half the evening holding Gemma,' Sebasten pointed out with amusement. 'I'm in the nursery in search of you.'

Already well-aware of that just from the smouldering gleam in his vibrant gaze as he surveyed her, Lizzie eased forward in a sinuous move into the hard heat and muscularity of his lean, powerful frame and gave him the most welcoming look of invitation she could manage.

'You're an incredible flirt,' Sebasten commented with satisfaction, surrendering at speed and scooping her up into his arms with an efficiency that spoke of regular practice.

'You like that...' Lizzie was used to being carried off to bed and ravished and she encouraged him in that shameless pursuit of pleasure every step of the way.

'I do. And carrying you around does keep me in the peak of athletic condition,' Sebasten teased as he settled her down on their bed.

Lizzie just laughed and kicked off her shoes. 'Kiss me and prove it.'

Sebasten pitched his jacket aside, dropped his tie where he stood, demonstrating an untidy streak that had once been foreign to him, and came down on the bed to haul her back into his arms. 'You're a wanton hussy and I adore you...'

Lizzie battered her eyelashes but the glow of her own love was there in her softened eyes for his to see. Before she could even tell him she loved him like crazy too, he released an appreciative groan in response to that look and melded her lush mouth to his own.

HARLEQUIN®

Super Romance®

*Looking for a romantic, emotional
and unforgettable escape?*

*You'll find it this month and every month
with a Harlequin Superromance!*

Rory Gorenzi has a sense of humor and a sense of
honor. She also happens to be good with children.

Seamus Lee, widower and father of four, needs
someone with exactly those traits.

They meet at the Colorado mountain school owned
by Rory's father, where she teaches skiing and
avalanche safety. But Seamus—and his children—
learn more from her than that....

Look for

GOOD WITH CHILDREN
by **Margot Early,**

*available August 2007, and these other
fantastic titles from Harlequin Superromance.*

REQUEST YOUR FREE BOOKS!

2 FREE NOVELS
PLUS 2
FREE GIFTS!

YES! Please send me 2 FREE Harlequin Presents® novels and my 2 FREE gifts. After receiving them, if I don't wish to receive any more books, I can return the shipping statement marked "cancel." If I don't cancel, I will receive 6 brand-new novels every month and be billed just $3.80 per book in the U.S., or $4.47 per book in Canada, plus 25¢ shipping and handling per book and applicable taxes, if any*. That's a savings of close to 15% off the cover price! I understand that accepting the 2 free books and gifts places me under no obligation to buy anything. I can always return a shipment and cancel at any time. Even if I never buy another book from Harlequin, the two free books and gifts are mine to keep forever.

106 HDN EEXK   306 HDN EEXV

Name	(PLEASE PRINT)

Address		Apt. #

City	State/Prov.	Zip/Postal Code

Signature (if under 18, a parent or guardian must sign)

Mail to the **Harlequin Reader Service®**:
IN U.S.A.: P.O. Box 1867, Buffalo, NY 14240-1867
IN CANADA: P.O. Box 609, Fort Erie, Ontario L2A 5X3

Not valid to current Harlequin Presents subscribers.

Want to try two free books from another line?
Call 1-800-873-8635 or visit www.morefreebooks.com.

* Terms and prices subject to change without notice. NY residents add applicable sales tax. Canadian residents will be charged applicable provincial taxes and GST. This offer is limited to one order per household. All orders subject to approval. Credit or debit balances in a customer's account(s) may be offset by any other outstanding balance owed by or to the customer. Please allow 4 to 6 weeks for delivery.

Your Privacy: Harlequin is committed to protecting your privacy. Our Privacy Policy is available online at www.eHarlequin.com or upon request from the Reader Service. From time to time we make our lists of customers available to reputable firms who may have a product or service of interest to you. If you would prefer we not share your name and address, please check here. ☐

HP07

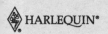

EVERLASTING LOVE™

Every great love has a story to tell™

A love story that distance and time has never dimmed.

While remodeling her home, April finds some old love letters addressed to Norma Marsh. Tracking down the owner, now in her eighties, brings to the surface secrets Norma has kept from her grandson Quinn, about a love close to her heart. A love April begins to understand as she starts to fall for Quinn…

Look for

A Secret To Tell You

by

Roz Denny Fox

On sale August 2007.

HARLEQUIN®

Mediterranean NIGHTS™

Glamour, elegance, mystery and revenge aboard the high seas...

Coming in August 2007...

THE TYCOON'S SON

by
award-winning author
Cindy Kirk

Businessman Theo Catomeris's long-estranged father is determined to reconnect with his son, so he hires Trish Melrose to persuade Theo to renew his contract with Liberty Line. Sailing aboard the luxurious *Alexandra's Dream* is a rare opportunity for the single mom to mix business and pleasure. But an undeniable attraction between Trish and Theo is distracting her from the task at hand....